To Rainbow Valley

Irene Bennett Brown

WISE WOLF
BOOKS

WISE WOLF BOOKS
An Imprint of Wolfpack Publishing
wisewolfbooks.com
701 S. Howard Ave. 106-324 Tampa, FL 33609

Cover design by Wise Wolf Books

Paperback ISBN 978-1-957548-80-7
eBook ISBN 978-1-957548-79-1

For my family with love; also for Alma Talmadge and Olive Rambo Cook, who helped my impossible dream to come true.

To Rainbow Valley

Chapter 1
The Dust and the Dream

Cotton Baldwin hunched on the milking stool with his head against the cow's hot, dusty flank trying not to hear the caterwauling wind outside. A worried look spread over his sun-darkened face as he stripped the last drops of milk into the half-full bucket. At each milking he got less. As he stood up, the barn door flew open and a cloud of dust swirled in before it banged shut again.

"It's Grandma," a hoarse voice choked out of the dimness. "You forgot the lids to the milk buckets. Bad enough to eat dust, we don't have to drink it!" his grandmother scolded. She came to the milk bench and pushed a lid down on each bucket.

Cotton frowned. "Pretty soon there won't be a need for lids," he said, wiping away the sweat that was running down his face, making mud as it mixed with the gritty dirt at the corners of his eyes and mouth. "Cows givin' less each day."

Grandma pushed back her dusty sunbonnet and

pulled down the cloth that had covered her nose and mouth. "Worst June since your Grandpa and I homesteaded here in 1890, more'n forty-five years ago. Used to be green grass waving as far as the eye could see. Air fresh and clean as a Monday wash, daisies blooming, orioles singing..." Grandma's voice softened as she remembered. A lump came to Cotton's throat as he could see it, too.

"Then the greedy fools plowed it up—for wheat they said." Grandma's eyes flashed. "An' now it's 1935 and West Kansas is just purely blowing away!"

"What if the wind doesn't stop?" Cotton asked bleakly.

"It'll stop. Always has. Going to rain again, too," Grandma said fiercely. "This can't last forever."

Cotton felt close to Grandma, listening to her talk in the murky heat of the barn. They'd come to live with her and help out after Grandpa died—but things just couldn't go on...

Grandma picked up one of the milk pails. "Bring the other when you've finished up. Don't think you'd make it with both hands full." She pulled the sunbonnet over her eyes, lifted the cloth over her nose, and left him.

Cotton hurried across the barn to the pig pen. Old Cannibal stood grunting on the far side, big and black as a bear. Cotton kept his eyes on Cannibal's gleaming tusks as he hung over the top rail and emptied the sour-smelling, watery feed into the trough below. Suddenly, the hog bolted across the pen and slashed wickedly. Cotton jerked out of reach just in time.

"Missed again!" he panted. "I wish you were a buffalo and I was an Indian. I'd take my Pawnee bow and—zing!" He stopped and grinned, shaking his head. "Maybe you're good for something. Most everything is, according to Mama." The hog noisily woof-woofed the trough empty while Cotton watched.

Cotton looked around and checked. Brindle and Bess were milked and fed, the stalls were cleaned, and Old Cannibal was taken care of. Unable to resist, he went to his old Peddler's box that sat close to the hay chute. What a guy Grandpa was to leave him this roomy chest to keep his stuff in, Cotton thought, unlocking it. As always, a mingled fragrance of gingham, spice, and tobacco arose as he opened the box, although it had held none of these things in the nearly fifty years since a horse and buggy merchant left the chest with Grandpa, never to return.

Carefully, as if it contained gold or a newborn baby, Cotton lifted a newspaper-wrapped bundle from the box. He unwrapped the parcel, his throat going full as it always did when he set eyes on the Pawnee bow and quiver. With a proud caress, he polished the jointed wood and bone of the short curved bow, tightened the buffalo sinew bowstring, then loosened it again. Grandpa's friend, Dr. Drake, had wanted the bow and quiver. His collection of Indian relics filled a whole room of his house in Willow Creek. But Grandpa had left the bow and quiver to him, Cotton.

"Got to get the milk to the house," he told himself. Reluctantly, he put the bow and quiver back in the

Peddler's box. Just looking at the bow, though, and touching it, was good medicine for a worried mind.

Closing the lid, Cotton snapped the padlock shut and hung the key in a secret place behind the chest. Even Ivy couldn't find it there. A nine-year-old sister could get pretty snoopy.

He pulled his blue bandanna handkerchief up over his mouth and nose and picked up the milk bucket.

For a moment he hesitated, his hand on the door latch, almost afraid. The old barn shook and creaked. Cotton sighed and lifted the latch, facing the fury of the storm.

The door jerked out of his hand as if it were alive and slammed against the barn. Dust stung his eyes. His mouth and nose filled with it in spite of the handkerchief. Finally he got the door latched. Chunks of earth sailed across the barnyard, still holding shoots of green wheat. Dad's crop, blowing right out of the ground again. Just like last year and the year before that. "Shouldn't us Baldwins do something this time besides complain?" Cotton asked himself bitterly.

Choking from the grit in his mouth he stepped into the wind. It pushed him to the house, whipping his overalls tightly about his legs. From under the porch an Australian shepherd dog poked his gray-blue spotted head out to look at Cotton, whining. "Better get back under there, Shag," Cotton yelled against the wind, staggering onto the porch. "Don't want you blowing off to Canada with the wheat." Tow-headed Ivy opened the door and bolted it after him. His mother looked up from stirring gravy at the stove, a smile of welcome lighting up her tired face for an instant.

"Dad home yet from Willa Creek?" Cotton asked, untying the handkerchief from around his neck and brushing dust from his sun-bleached hair. He stepped wide over his little brother Bobby, and the baby, Kurt, playing with clothespins on the kitchen floor.

Ivy, a grin on her pixie face, draped a clean ragged dishtowel around her shoulders. "The Pater has not arrived," she said grandly.

Cotton snorted disdainfully and started around her to the back room where he slept, hoping to read a chapter or two before supper.

"Wait, Son," Mama said. "Help Ivy finish stuffing rags around the windows. Please. Daisy's about to smother from the dust."

Cotton turned. His book, Call of the Wild, lay on his bed. His biggest dream was to have exciting adventures like those Jack London wrote about, but it was almost as good to read them. You'd have to leave your family if you did things like that.

A series of rasping coughs came from the cot on the far side of the room. Cotton's shoulders sagged. Daisy, only two years younger than he, seemed to get a little smaller with each dust storm. It couldn't be much fun, being sick most of the time. He grabbed a cloth from Ivy. "Sure, Mama," he said. He'd read the book three times, anyway.

"It's time we left this dusty old place!" Cotton stormed as he worked. "First it's tornadoes—making us high-tail it for the root cellar out back. Then it's dust storms and we have to stuff every little crack to keep out the dust. It doesn't make a lick of sense!"

From her rocking chair Grandma Baldwin raised her voice against the keening wind outside. "That's what's wrong with folks—want to run from their troubles. Nobody wants to stand up and face 'em anymore." She got up and began taking dishes from the cupboard, wiping dust from each with a dishtowel. "Life ain't all sunshine," she shook a cup at Cotton. "You'll find that out."

Dad's arrival interrupted. He hurried inside as Cotton opened the door, then slammed it shut against the shrieking wind and dust that poured in.

Cotton examined his father's face anxiously. It was grayer than it should have been, even from the dust. Dad gave his cap to Ivy. He shoved his hands deep into the pockets of his faded overalls and was silent for a moment.

Finally, he spoke. "The bank can't loan us another cent," he said soberly. "Not even enough for more seed. There isn't a shoot of this year's crop left in the ground. I was just out there looking."

Cotton drew in his breath, waiting.

"What will we do, Preston?" Cotton's mother cried. "We need food and Daisy has to have medicine. How will we live?"

Dad frowned, worry etching deep lines in his face. He shook his head. Mama went into his arms, and he patted her shoulder. Cotton watched, wanting desperately to help. "We could go out West!" he blurted. "That's what the pioneers did when they weren't satisfied with where they lived." Dad gave him a sharp look. Cotton's ears turned warm.

His father's dusty face broke into a slow grin. "Not a bad idea at all," he said with a lift in his voice. He gave Mama's shoulder a last gentle pat as she turned back to the stove. "I've been thinking that myself lately. My family deserves a better life than this. School's out. It would be a good time to make a change."

Cotton's heart beat rapidly. Dad was serious. Go West! He hadn't been farther than Willa' Creek—ten miles. Immediately he was thinking about what he'd take—the Pawnee bow and quiver, his Jack London book, his collection of arrowheads, his string of sleigh bells-

Suddenly he was jerked back to the present. Grandma was riled for certain. He cringed as she slammed down a plate and pounded the table with her fist. Cotton hoped the coal-oil lamp in the center of the table wouldn't upset.

"Some troubles just got to be lived with," she declared. "In case nobody around here knows it, that's a fact."

"No, Grandma," Dad said gently. "It's wrong to put up with some of them. In time folks will figure out how to fight dust and drought. Maybe they'll plant the prairie back to buffalo grass. But we can't wait." He brushed his forehead with the back of his hand. "It isn't that I'm not proud of you and Papa," he went on. "I'm very proud. You stayed with the land through thick and thin. But," a deep sadness came into his face, "I'm remembering how Papa got lost in a dust storm on his farm and died two weeks later of dust pneumonia."

Cotton followed his father's glance to where Daisy lay coughing. Cold dread washed over him. Not Daisy —she couldn't—

Grandma's mouth shut in a grim line. She crossed to the stove and dipped into a bowl of broth. Her chin trembled as she settled in the cane-bottom chair by the girl's bed. The tin spoon tapped the sides of the white bowl as she helped Daisy eat. "You know I love this girl. I worry about her, too. But leavin' Kansas is somethin' else again."

The silence was long. Ivy leaned against Cotton's chair and for once, Cotton was glad to have her near. Grown-up problems made him uncomfortable. Mama's face had a tight, worried look as she took a platter of side meat from the warming oven and called them to eat.

"It's the only thing we can do, Grandma," Dad spoke finally when they were seated. He looked across the table at Cotton and smiled. "Seems like our thinking has been running neck and neck today, like a good team. If you want to go West," he asked, "how about Oregon?"

Cotton swallowed the hardness in his throat. "Oregon!" he cried gleefully. "Why, Oregon's practically a wilderness. Wild animals out there and everything. High mountains. Lots of big trees." He gripped the edge of the table, laughing. "I guess we'd all like that!"

"I saw Tom Hammond today," Dad continued.

"The Hammonds are moving to Oregon, a place called Gladrock."

Cotton waited breathlessly as his father hesitated, then continued, "Mrs. Hammond's cousin wrote to them from Oregon. She said there are jobs out there."

He turned to Mama. "I guess we could help turn those big trees Cotton's talking about into lumber, pick fruit, work in a cannery, or on a regular farm. What do you think, Veri?"

Mama's eyes were bright. She reached out and grasped Dad's arm. "Oh, Pres, it sounds wonderful. It would be so good for Daisy to get away from the dust."

Dad frowned as he slowly sipped his coffee. "It wouldn't be easy, Veri," he said. "But it would be worth anything to find a better life for you and the youngsters and Grandma. Hammonds say I could ride out there with them, work a while, then send for the rest of you." He sighed deeply. "The big problem is, could you manage without me?"

Ivy threw her sun-browned arms around her brother. "Cotton could do it, Daddy—he could take care of us—couldn't you, Cotton?" she squealed.

Cotton pushed Ivy's wispy blond locks away from his face and glared at her. Now why did the little goof have to say that? The others were watching him. He squirmed, scratched his nose, examined the brass fastener of his suspender. 'Course he wanted to go, more than anything. But could he take care of everybody till Dad sent for them?

Chapter 2
Cotton In Charge

Cotton's father broke the silence around the table. "With luck I may find work right away. What do you think, Cotton? If I left you in charge, could you take care of things?"

"M-m-me?" Cotton stammered. Part of him glowed —Dad was asking him to take his place. In the pit of him, though, fear was brewing. "Do you mean take care of everything?" he gulped.

"The whole kit n kaboodle," Dad nodded. "Chores, helping your mother with the heavy work and getting things ready for the trip. Of course I'd tune up the Chevy before I go. You'd have to be head scout all the way to Oregon."

Cotton searched his mind for an answer. Suddenly, the cane-bottom chair on the other side of the room crashed to the floor. Grandma was on her feet. "Wet-nosed puppy," she stormed, shaking the spoon at Dad. "That's what George is. Never thought I'd see the day a body would think of turning over a farm and family, lock, stock, and barrel, to a young'un only thirteen years old."

Cotton's mouth fell open. Grandma never called him George unless she was angry. Because of his white hair, almost everybody called him Cotton. A wet-nosed puppy! Him, Cotton? The blood in his head began to throb hotly. His chest rose and fell. Squaring his shoulders, he jabbed his thumbs under the suspenders of his overalls. Looking Dad in the eye, he blurted, "I can do it, Dad! You can count on me."

Three days later, Cotton wasn't so sure. The dust storm was over, for a while anyway, leaving the countryside looking like an ocean of dirt-colored waves under a clear blue sky. Dad had left for Oregon only that morning.

Starting on the evening chores, Cotton remembered that he had felt like bawling with the others when Dad got into the Hammonds' car. But a guy in charge...

He listened to the windmill whirring in a light wind and held himself a little straighter as he padded barefoot through the dust, Shag trotting at his side. He'd do his best in Dad's place. He'd given his word.

As he entered the barn, the warm, fragrant smell of hay and cows filled Cotton's nostrils. On an impulse, he decided to feed Old Cannibal before he milked. He always felt better when Cannibal was taken care of for the night.

Filling the bucket from the swill barrel, Cotton

carried it back to the pen. Good, the big hog was outside, asleep in the shadow of the barn. Quickly sloshing the mixture into the trough, he stood well back from the rails around the pen and called, "Soo—eee, soo—eee." The hog charged up the ramp into the pen. His noisy slurping and woofing as he ate made Cotton grin.

"Hog!" Cotton accused, laughing.

He turned away and got his three-legged milking stool and clean milk pail. Bess and Brindle waited in their stanchions, quietly chewing the ration of hay and sorghum silage he'd given them earlier. He shoved the stool behind him and sat down with his head near Brindle's warm flank. Cotton sent the milk drumming into the pail which he held firmly between his knees.

Time passed quickly and he soon realized he had all the milk he was going to get this time. He placed the buckets carefully on the waist-high shelf nailed to the side wall. Grandma'd complain plenty that he hadn't gotten more—but she wouldn't admit they ought to leave Kansas.

Cotton turned the cows out of the barn, cleaned their stalls, then stood silent, listening. Mice rustled in the loft. Out near the pasture gate an oriole sang loud and sweet. No Cannibal noises, though. He hurried to the pig pen with the shovel. The pen was empty. Cannibal was stretched out again in the shadow of the barn.

Sweat ran down Cotton's face in little rivers as he worked. "Got to get out of here quick as I can," he panted to Shag, who lay watching outside the pen. "No telling what that critter would do if he caught me here." Push, lift, push, lift—it was almost done. Suddenly, Cotton heard an ugly grunting close behind him. Prickles raced up his spine. He whirled to look. Old Cannibal lunged through the doorway like a pre-historic monster bent on destruction. Cotton's muscles tensed for action. As the hog charged, he leaped for the gate into the barn and plunged through, jerking it shut behind him. He stood there, quivering. "That does it!" he choked out. "We've had some ornery hogs, but you're the orneriest! And I'm through worryin' you're going to take a chunk out of my backside!"

He hurried through the rest of his chores, raced to the house, and blurted his plan.

"No sir, you can't sell that hog," Grandma stormed, rocking furiously by the window. "We don't know that Preston will find work out there. That hog's all we got to eat this winter."

"But, Grandma," Cotton persisted, "we could use the money to go to Dad in Oregon. It'd help a lot. And Dad won't give up and come home, will he, Mama?"

She shook her head. "No, I don't think he will, Son. If you could find a buyer, we could surely use the money for the trip. Times are hard, though. Dollar bills are as scarce as hen's teeth."

Cotton sighed, satisfied. When Mama used that tone, a matter was the same as settled. Although he wanted to stay up and help explain things to Grandma so she'd understand, Mama sent him to bed.

A few weeks later, Cotton walked down the lane from their farm to the county road, Shag at his heels.

Cotton lifted his too-big straw hat, a hand-me-down from his father, wiped the sweat from his forehead, and set the hat back on.

"Mama's right," he thought irritably. "Selling Old Cannibal ain't easy." For days and days he'd been trying. A telephone would make it easier. He could just ring up the neighbors an' ask if they would like to buy a hog.

"Lot of good that'd do," he mumbled aloud. "I wouldn't know how to use the thing an' the answer would still be no money.'"

Cotton felt a jolt of surprise much later. He had come far—ahead was Joe Swap's "farm." Anticipation raced through him. Joe's several acres were never planted to a crop. Instead, in a large circle around a few tumble-down buildings, Joe's land sprouted rusty fenders, engines, horse collars, rickety wagons— everything.

He'd better not stop. Joe only traded. He wouldn't have money to buy Cannibal. That's what he was out here for, to sell the hog. On the other hand, exploring Joe Swap's place was close to real adventure. He liked Joe. "C'mon," Cotton beckoned to Shag as he turned into the lane.

The noonday sun beat down, glancing off bits of glass and metal here and there with eye-hurting brilliance. Cotton found Joe napping on a bursting horsehair sofa set in the meager shade of a water-hungry hackberry tree. Cotton grinned.

Joe Swap looked like a Santa Claus in overalls who'd somehow gotten lost from his rightful place in the North. Only one suspender was fastened over his shoulder—Joe wasn't one to bother with unnecessary details and one suspender held up his overalls just fine.

Cotton cleared his throat and tapped the old man's chest. "Hello, Mr. Swap. I'm Cotton Baldwin. I came to see you."

The round eyes in the wrinkled old face popped open and squinted at Cotton. "Hullo," he nodded. "Git out of the sun. Sit on the ground there." He sat up, blinking. "You come out in this heat just to visit an old feller like me?" he asked, obviously pleased.

Cotton sat down cross-legged in the shade. He nodded. "Partly that. I'm out trying to sell Old Cannibal, our hog. Dad's gone to Oregon. He's going to find work out there, then send for the rest of us."

Joe stretched. "Nice place, Oregawn," he said.

Cotton nodded with enthusiasm, then, curiosity getting the better of him, he got up and peeked into a mildewed trunk. It was empty. He moved on to finger a worn-out, dust-coated saddle. Suddenly, he stopped. He must be dreaming. "What's this?" he asked.

Joe snorted. "A rowboat, same as it looks." He chuckled. "It's the funniest thing I ever traded fer. Some tenderfoot folks from Minniesoda came out here in March, when ponds're full. They started building that 'scow' they called it. I'd have give a buffalo nickel to have seen their faces when they got that boat done about the time the ponds dried up. I thought the whole world knowed western Kansas ain't got any water nine-tenths of the year." He shook with laughter. "I keep it aroun' just fer laughs," he choked. " 'Course nobody has ever wanted it."

"I do," Cotton said suddenly. "I want it for going to Oregon."

Joe Swap stumbled over to Cotton. "Looka' here, boy," he said kindly, "you ain't going to get to Oregawn in no rowboat!"

Cotton grinned. "I know that, Mr. Swap," he said. "But it looks to me like I could use it as a trailer, to haul our stuff in to Oregon. It would hold all the blankets, food, dishes, and things Mama needs to take. Then when we get to Oregon, Dad and I can use it for fishing."

Cotton cringed as Joe Swap pounded his back. "That's a good idear!" Joe exclaimed. "You got a brain under all that white hair. Yessir, but ain't you gonna need wheels?"

Cotton laughed modestly and hitched up his overalls. "Couldn't you fix up a sort of boat trailer from parts of these old cars?" he asked.

Joe Swap looked and his eyes gleamed. "What you got to swap?" he asked quickly.

"Cannibal, our hog. Over five hundred pounds of pork. Salted down and smoked, it'd last you a long time, Mr. Swap."

The old man's eyes twinkled. "Throw in that Pawnee bow yer Pa told me about honest?"

A shiver ran through Cotton. He shook his head. Not the bow! "I—I couldn't," he stammered. "My Grandpa left it to me when he died. And I—I may be able to use it in Oregon." How could he make Joe

Swap see how it was about the bow and quiver, the most special things in his life? Grandpa once saved Chief Keola's people from starving—by giving some of his own cows to them. The Pawnee Chief gave Grandpa the bow and quiver to show his appreciation.

"Don't look so scairt," Joe Swap's voice broke into his thoughts. "I was just funnin' ya. I'll swap you the boat for the hog, straight across."

Cotton heaved a deep sigh. "Thanks a lot, Mr. Swap. Thanks!"

An hour later he was home. He burst through the door, eager to tell his news. The nutlike fragrance of beans cooking with pork greeted him and his stomach churned with hunger. At the table, Grandma and Mama sat piecing quilt blocks. Daisy, pretty and pale in a faded green dress, sat between them. She smiled and Cotton answered with a triumphant grin.

"I did it," his voice was almost a shout, "I got rid of Old Cannibal!"

"Oh, good!" Mama exclaimed, jumping to her feet and grabbing him by the shoulders.

Grandma shook her head. "We're going to need that hog come winter. Preston'll be back to stay I tell you."

"But, Grandma," Cotton began.

Mama interrupted, shaking him. "How much, Son?" she asked, her eyes shining. "Who bought him?"

"Nobody. I traded him for a boat," Cotton said.

Mama's hands dropped as though suddenly weighted by stone. Everybody stared open-mouthed at him, as if he had said he had climbed a beanstalk and killed a giant. "A boat," he said into the quiet room. "Never been used. A green boat."

"A green boat!" Grandma was suddenly on her feet, screaming. "A green boat!" She waved her arms. Bits of colored cloth fluttered every which way like frightened butterflies. "This young 'un has been eating loco weed!"

Mama shushed the older woman, then cleared her throat. She looked very white. "Now, what is this, Son? Why would you trade Cannibal for a boat? There're no lakes or rivers for miles; even the well is about dry."

"For Oregon," Cotton said. His heart beat very fast. "Joe Swap is going to make us a boat trailer. You can put all your things in it, Mama. You too, Grandma. I wanted it mostly for you—so you wouldn't have to leave your things behind. It will be the same as pulling a regular trailer, only after we get to Oregon, we'll have the boat for fishing."

They looked stunned. Finally Grandma spoke. "Get a stick, Veri, this boy needs a walloping."

Cotton looked at Mama, dumbfounded. She shook her head, then smiled. "The boat is a good idea," she said to Grandma. "He tried awfully hard to sell the hog but nobody could buy it. When you stop to think about it, the boat will be handy."

Grandma started to interrupt but Mama went on. "We should have waited, though, until Pres wrote to us. The boat will be useless if we're not going to Oregon. I'm proud of you, Cotton, for doing what you could, but it's best you tell Joe we can't honor his bargain until we know."

Cotton's shoulders dropped. A heavy feeling began to grow inside him. He'd have to tell Joe not to build the trailer. His good idea suddenly seemed worthless. He turned blindly and went to do the chores.

Chapter 3
The Letter

Although birds were singing early the next morning as Cotton headed for Joe Swap's place, he didn't feel happy. The grizzled old man was busy on the boat trailer. Cotton's heart sank even further. "H'lo Mr. Swap. Deal's off," Cotton said quietly. He watched a wide grin disappear from the whiskery face. Cotton kicked at the ground as he explained. "I'm sorry you've already done so much on the trailer," he finished.

The old man straightened and nodded. After a while, he spoke. "Boy, do you think yer Pa's going to send for you one of these days?"

Cotton was surprised. "Sure! Dad's finished with hard times. We'll get a letter one of these days, saying for us to come to Oregon."

Joe's eyes snapped. "Then I'll take a chance and finish this here trailer. No need to tell yer women. They'll just get panicky. When the letter comes, I'll bring the boat over an' get the hog."

Cotton blinked. The sun hitting on the stuff in the yard sure was bright today. "That's swell, Mr. Swap. I'll let you know when the letter comes."

Going home, Cotton's legs ached with weariness. Hot dust seemed to be broiling into his skin. Inside though, he felt good. He'd have to be careful not to show it. Grandma would suspect something, sure.

As he neared the lane to the house, his gaze fastened on the mailbox squatting across the road in a clump of dusty buffalo grass. His heart began to pound. The little metal flag was up, glinting in the sun. It was past time for the mailman to come—so he had left something in the box!

Cotton began to run. "Better not be an old advertisement," he hissed between his teeth. He jerked open the mailbox door. With shaking fingers he picked up the thin white envelope that lay inside. The return address read, Preston H. Baldwin, Rural Route 2, Gladrock, Oregon. Dad.

Cotton raced up the lane to the house, his bare feet stirring up a dust cloud in his trail. He plunged through the open door and crashed into the table in the middle of the room.

Grandma jumped up and stared. Mama came hurrying from the back room, the baby on her hip.

Cotton held out the letter. "Mama," he gasped. "Letter. Letter from Dad!"

Cotton gripped the back of a chair. Mama's fingers shook as she tore open the letter. Ivy, Daisy, and Bobby appeared from nowhere. Grandma's chin was sticking out stubbornly but her eyes looked worried.

Cotton knew she'd be glad if Dad had written to say he couldn't find work and was coming home. Otherwise...

" 'Dear folks,' " his mother began to read, " I have been lucky. I've found a job managing the dandiest little farm you ever set eyes on!"

Cotton leaped into the air. "Yieee," he war whooped happily. Mama waved for silence and went on. " It's a regular farm, with eleven cows, pigs, chickens, even a couple of geese. Our real living will come from several acres of peach trees. The main barn is built well, but the house is old. It does have lots of room, though, twelve rooms in all. This is the greenest country I've ever seen, no dust. Veri, hon, wish you could see the flowers in the yard. They are every color of the rainbow. Which reminds me—"

Mama stopped reading and wiped her eyes with her apron. She continued, " 'The town is located in Rainbow Valley. Seems like an omen to me. If we can work things out, I know us Baldwins have finally found the pot of gold at the end of the rainbow."

Cotton felt like yelling, he was so happy, but Mama wasn't finished.

" 'There's one drawback—' " she read.

"I knew it." Grandma nodded triumphantly.

"Wait, Grandma," Cotton pleaded. "Go ahead, Mama."

" '—There's one drawback," Mama continued. " 'Our food comes straight from our farm, and we have a roof. But my wages won't come until the peaches are picked and I collect my share from that. That means I won't have any cash to send you, to pay your way out here. And I need all of you here, to pick, by the middle of August. That's two weeks. After that, the peaches will be too ripe. I've been thinking if you had an auction, sold everything in the place except what we need, like pots and pans, you could probably raise enough cash to come. Maybe Cotton could find out if Joe Swap has a trailer."

"Already have," Cotton nodded, grinning. "Wait till Dad finds out about the boat. What else does Dad say, Mama?" he asked.

"He says he wishes he could hug all of us, thinks of us all the time, and hopes we're getting along okay." She smiled.

"I'll take care of everything, Mama," Cotton promised.

"And I'll answer your father's letter, telling him to expect us. I'll tell him we'll try very hard to get there in time." She nodded, suddenly looking eager to be gone.

"We'll be in Oregon in no time," Cotton assured her. He turned away quickly. He didn't want to do something dumb, like kiss somebody, but he sure felt good. As he turned, he tripped and almost fell over the baby, Kurt. He reached down, picked him up and threw the one-year-old into the air. Laughter gurgled from the small pink lips as the baby sailed upward. His blue eyes sparkled. Cotton caught him, held his chubby body close, and waltzed around the room. "We're going to cross the big, big mountains," Cotton singsonged. "And cross rivers, and deserts and—and then we'll get to Oregon where Dad is!"

Four-year-old Bobby broke the happy spell that

filled the room. "Where's Grandma?" he asked solemnly.

Cotton stopped twirling. He looked at his mother questioningly.

Mama shook her head. "It's awfully hard for her— leaving her home. I think she's gone for a walk, to think. When she comes back let's all be especially nice to her."

Cotton nodded. Grandma and Grandpa had worked hard to turn a section of wild prairie into the farm. Fighting drought, dust storms, and grasshoppers. Those things were bad, but she was used to them. This new place they were going to would be strange for all of them. That's probably why she was afraid to leave Kansas. Poor Grandma.

Cotton hugged the baby tighter, then put him on the floor. "After dinner," he said soberly, "I'll go over to Mr. Sather's place and ask him to auction for us."

On the way home, after getting Mr. Sather's okay, Cotton turned into Joe Swap's farm. "Got the letter!" he yelled, seeing the old man poking around through a pile of rusted hardware. "It was there when I got home. We're going to Oregon for sure. Dad's got a swell place."

The little man clapped Cotton's back. "S'fine! I knew yer daddy wouldn't let ya down."

A huge grin spread across Cotton's face. "Boat trailer going to take long? You can come get Cannibal anytime."

"Coupla' days, maybe." The old man looked wise. "I'm fixin' a s'prise for ya" Cotton started to protest but

Joe held up his hands. "Now don't badger me. Run along home. A s'prise is a s'prise."

In bed that night, Cotton's heart was light. The auction was set for Tuesday. In a day or two Joe would bring the boat and take Cannibal off his hands. They were going to Oregon, really going! He wondered what Joe's surprise might be, then pushed it from his mind and went to sleep.

The day came, and Cotton ran to meet Joe's pickup as it rattled up the lane. War whooping like an Indian, he skidded past the halted pickup to stare at the boat and trailer fastened behind. His heart pounded. "You cleaned it up swell, Mr. Swap." Cotton ran his fingers along the shiny green prow. "Trailer looks like straight from a factory!"

"I done the writin' myself," Joe boasted, pointing to wobbly letters that staggered along the side of the boat.

"Oregon Or Dust," Cotton read, snickering. Joe was pretty smart!

"That's yer s'prise, Cotton boy," the old man laughed with him. "I done wrote a sayin' to get ya' to Oregon. Oregon or dust, that's yer choice."

A short time later, Cotton stood by the battered truck peering through the rails at Old Cannibal. Loading the hog, with Joe's help, hadn't been too bad. The hog was quiet and seemed content. "Bye, old varmint," Cotton said. "You're doing us Baldwins a favor, helping us get to Oregon. We're going to remember you the rest of our lives for that."

Tuesday morning Cotton opened his eyes before

dawn, stretched, and leaped out of bed. He reached eagerly for his overalls draped over a chair. The past few days had whirled by with the speed of a dust devil. It was sale day, their last day in Kansas. Almost everything not for sale was packed and ready to be stowed in the boat.

Before leaving the room Cotton took the Pawnee bow and quiver from where he'd hung them by the door the night before. He'd pack them carefully. Lucky they had the boat so they'd have room for special things, like the bow. He ran his hand lightly over the beads and quills decorating the quiver, and along the silky curve of the bow. Then he put them on his bed.

Mama was already bustling about the kitchen as he entered, stirring a steaming kettle of cornmeal mush on the stove, and putting bowls on the table.

"Morning, Mama," he said. She answered with a warm smile, her eyes dancing with excitement.

"Hurry with your breakfast, Son," she said. "We have a lot yet to do before folks start coming. I'm so glad Joe came yesterday for the hay. I think he bought it mostly to help us out—heaven knows where he got the cash—but he insisted he wanted the hay for 'tradin' purposes."

Cotton grinned and went out to the back porch. As he splashed his face with water from the basin on the wash bench, he thought about Joe and the hay. Would they find folks as good as Joe in Oregon? He returned to the kitchen. "Ivy and me can carry the rest of the stuff out to the yard as soon as chores are done. Bobby can help with the little stuff," he told his mother.

She sighed wistfully as she filled his bowl. "I suppose it won't take long. We don't have much. I wish we did, so we'd get more money. Then, on the other hand, I don't like parting with anything..."

Everything but the heavy kitchen stove stood in the yard by nine-thirty. Looking around as he rubbed his tired arms, Cotton decided that the table, beds, and chairs looked shabbier somehow, outside. Grandma's rocker sat still and empty in the dust. Since the day the letter came, she hadn't said much to anyone.

The sound of a car coming up the lane made Cotton turn. It was Mr. Sather. For the next hour, Cotton followed the lanky auctioneer around.

Companionably, they regrouped the household goods, decided on a spot to show Brindle and Bess, and piled some rusty machinery. Shortly afterward, a stream of jalopies filled the air with dust as they rattled up the lane and chugged to a stop before the barn. Almost everyone carried a dishtowel-covered bowl or pan—food for the picnic that would be held after the auction.

A shiver of alarm raced up Cotton's spine when he saw Dr. Drake's Model-A Ford slowly chugging up the lane. If Dr. Drake was coming for the bow and quiver, he'd just have to let him know they weren't for sale.

At that moment, the auctioneer pointed a bony finger. "Bring that Brindle cow over here, Son," he said.

Cotton led Brindle forward, stroking her warm side as he did so. The auctioneer's chant rang out, causing the voices to quiet. After a while, Cotton saw a red-faced farmer in a straw hat pull his earlobe in a signal to Mr. Sathers.

"Got ten, who'll gimme 'leven," the auctioneer chanted.

Ten dollars! Cotton couldn't believe it. Ten dollars was a lot of money, but at that rate they'd never get enough to go to Oregon.

The auctioneer chanted on, but a higher bid didn't come. Cotton studied the blank faces in the crowd with disbelief.

"Going, going, go-i-ing, gone to that red-faced man in the straw hat!" Mr. Sathers shouted finally.

"Give you twenty-two fifty for both cows," the red-faced farmer yelled out.

"Sold!" cried the auctioneer.

"Mama," Cotton asked, finding her on the edge of the crowd a short time after, "what will we do? We're not getting enough money."

She shook her head tiredly and put her arm across his shoulders. "They're our friends and neighbors. They're here to help us if they can. But they have precious little money to spare."

"We have to get enough money to get to Oregon and help Dad harvest the peaches," Cotton persisted, following her to the house. Inside, he watched her go to a pile of belongings set aside for the trip. She picked up a large square bundle, carefully wrapped in a clean white sheet. "Mama, what're you doing?" Her chin quivered and he knew. "No, Mama! Not your wedding ring quilt!" As long as he could remember she had kept it put away for "when good times come."

"Yes," she said, in a stone-cool voice. "Your Pawnee bow and quiver, too, Son. I'm sure Dr. Drake will bid a good price for them—he's wanted them for his collection since Grandpa had them."

"Mama!" Cotton's voice was full of the shock he felt. "You don't mean—?"

She nodded, her eyes filling with tears. "I know how you feel, Son. You've never had a bicycle, or a horse of your own—just the Pawnee bow. But we must sell everything we don't absolutely need."

Cotton stared at the quilt. Inside, he felt like ice was breaking up, then freezing again.

Mama went on in a low voice. "Whatever money the bow and quiver bring, it's yours to carry. We won't use it unless an emergency comes up—I think we'll have almost enough without it. If we don't need it, the money will be yours when we get to Oregon. All right?"

Cotton couldn't answer. Was he having a horrible nightmare? He couldn't believe he was actually getting the bow and quiver and taking them outside. But he was.

By noon, everything was sold except some odds and ends nobody bid on, including Grandma's rocker. These they gave to friends.

Cotton moved numbly through the crowd, not seeing, not caring. In his pocket a crisp ten-dollar bill was clenched in his fist. How glad everybody was, how lucky they thought he was, when Dr. Drake bid ten dollars for the bow and quiver. But they didn't know!

He stumbled to the barn, climbed to the empty loft, and lay on his back staring blindly at the cobwebs above him. Outside, he could hear the talk and laughter of the men setting up sawhorses and boards for a picnic table. The clink of dishes mixed with the chatter of the women and girls. "I'll sock the first person that comes up that ladder and tells me to come eat," he vowed angrily.

The bow. A shudder, almost like a sob, shook his frame from head to toe. Now he really knew how Grandma felt about the farm. To her, the farm was probably like part of Grandpa. The bow was like that. When he looked at it and the quiver, he could almost see Grandpa's face. The crinkly eyes that seemed to shoot off sparks, the snowy mustache that was always turned up with a grin. He closed his eyes and could almost hear Grandpa telling him the stories again, about how it was in Kansas back in Indian times. They ought to keep the bow—keep it in the family always, just because it had been Grandpa's.

Cotton smacked the floor hard with his palm, causing a few scraggles of hay to dance into the air. "I'm not going to do it," he hissed aloud. "Grandpa left the bow to me. It's up to me to decide." He rushed down the ladder and outside, fast before he could change his mind.

He found Dr. Drake sitting in the shade, at the corner of the house. Resting in the doctor's lap was a plate heaped with golden fried chicken, biscuits and wild grape preserves, hominy, and a large slice of molasses pie.

Cotton knelt in front of him. "I want to buy the bow and quiver back," he whispered urgently.

The doctor's bushy-white brows shot up. He waved a drumstick for Cotton to sit down.

Cotton sat beside him, wishing it were over with. "It's this way—" he began. Cotton repeated what he'd been thinking in the barn. When he finished the doctor's capable old hand patted the patched spot on his knee.

"A boy ought to be able to keep a souvenir of his heritage," Dr. Drake said gruffly. "The bow and quiver's in the rumble seat of my coupe. If you ever want to sell—"

A glow spread through Cotton like fire. He could keep the bow! He leaped to his feet and tossed the money toward the doctor's lap. The bill landed on the doctor's pie.

Dr. Drake grunted with good-natured disgust.

"Sorry," Cotton grinned. Suddenly he had an idea. "I have a Peddler's box Grandpa gave me," he said quickly. "It's too heavy to take to Oregon and nobody bought it. I want you to have it." Dr. Drake reached toward his pocket but Cotton shook his head. "No," he cleared his throat, "you were Grandpa's friend." He turned away, shoved his hands deep into his pockets, and moved slowly through the crowd. It seemed hours before he reached the doctor's car.

Chapter 4
The Journey Begins

That night Cotton lay under his blankets on the bare floor of the empty house. He was sure nobody saw him hide the bow and quiver kitty corner under the back seat of the Chevy. They were safe there. So why did he feel bad?

Because Mama doesn't have her wedding ring quilt anymore, the voice of his conscience seemed to answer. Grandma can't ever again rock away her mad spells in her rocking chair. And you have the bow and quiver.

Cotton tossed restlessly, trying to escape the voice in his mind.

Wasn't it right to keep something? A souvenir of Kansas and all the years the family lived here? A new thought came to him and he lay more quietly. Whatever happened from now until they reached Oregon, he'd fix it up himself, so they wouldn't need the bow money. "I can do it, I know I can," he whispered aloud. "It was right I kept the bow."

"What did you say, Son?" his mother's voice asked sleepily.

Cotton stiffened. "N-nothing, Mama," he answered.

He woke the next morning feeling a dull soreness along his back and legs. He turned stiffly on his side and opened his eyes. He was on the floor—now why —? Wednesday. That was it. Today they were leaving for Oregon!

After a quick breakfast, Cotton carried the rolled bedding out to the boat. He packed the food box where it would be easy to reach. Besides the picnic food left over from sale day, they had a bag of potatoes and one of onions, some canned goods, and flour and mixings for biscuits and pancakes. It was almost as though they were going out on a long picnic. Probably be as much fun as one, he told himself, his heart high.

Cotton checked and rechecked his load. Four cardboard cartons were packed, holding clothing, towels, dishes, pots and pans, and other things they'd need. The coal oil lantern was in. Cotton started to the house for matches. Suddenly he remembered he hadn't seen Shag for quite a while. They didn't want to forget him.

"Here, Shag, here, boy," he called. He got the matches and put them into the food box. He looked around, but Shag hadn't come. "Here, boy," he yelled again. "C'mon, Shag, hurry up for corn sake!"

He covered the boat with a tarp, drawing it over the load, then lashed it on with a rope, leaving room in the prow for Shag. Cotton looked up and his heartbeat quickened with pride. Bobby and Kurt came toward

him, well-combed and clean in fresh cotton sunsuits. Daisy and Ivy looked as if they were dressed for a party. Mama was right handy at turning printed flour sacks into clothes. He glanced at Grandma, then quickly looked away from the misery in her eyes.

"All ready?" Mama called, closing and locking the door of the little gray house for the last time.

"No, Mama, Shag isn't here." Cotton nervously scratched his head. He whistled shrilly for Shag.

They waited as Cotton called and whistled, again and again. "Maybe something has happened to him," Cotton worried aloud. He paced the yard.

"Oh, Son, you know how Shag is," Mama said, exasperation in her voice. "Sometimes he stays out all day chasing rabbits."

Mama was right. He should have remembered that about Shag and tied him up so he wouldn't leave. Now it was too late. Angry at himself, he was afraid they might have to go without Shag.

As though reading his mind, Mama spoke, "We'll have to go on without him."

"No," Cotton blurted, "he'll be all alone here! He'll come back and wonder where I am." Cotton looked into his mother's eyes, pleading. "Please, Mama, we can't leave him behind. Who would look after him?"

"I've thought it out," Mama answered. She placed an arm across his shoulders. "We'll stop and ask Joe Swap to find Shag, then keep him. Joe is a good man. I'm sure he'd like having Shag for company."

Loss and disappointment dragged at Cotton's heart as he moved slowly to the car. "All right," he said in an

empty voice. What could he do? He had the bow and quiver. Could he ask for the whole world besides? Yet, as he climbed into the car beside Grandma, it was all he could do to keep from shouting, "No! No! We can't go without Shag!"

When Mama turned the car from the lane onto the county road, Cotton looked back. He knew that as long as he lived he'd never forget the sightless windows of the empty house, the wind-swept, dusty yard, the creaking windmill with no one to grease the gears. And his dog, though he wasn't really there, waiting for him by the porch. Cotton scrunched back in the seat, pressing his arms against the sickness growing in his stomach.

Later, heading up the lane to Joe Swap's place, he forced a grin. Joe stuck his grizzled head through the open window. "I can have your dog?" he chortled. "I'll take good care of him, boy. I'll go looking for him right off." The old man's eyes grew misty. "Gonna miss you folks," his voice quavered. "Wish you didn't have to go. But you young 'uns going to grow up to be real fine folks in that Oregon country. Shur as shootin'."

A new thought struck Cotton as the car rolled on toward Willow Creek. They might see Shag yet. He looked, but saw nothing except miles of barren land, and above, gigantic castle-like clouds floating in a million more acres of blue sky.

At the small, sunbaked town of Willow Creek, Cotton followed the red-haired service station attendant about as he checked the car thoroughly, filled the gasoline tank, and changed the oil. When he was finished, Cotton asked, "S'pose I can have a map of Colorado and Utah?"

The man grinned at the boat with "Oregon or Dust" painted on the side. He kicked the left trailer wheel. "Going west to Oregon, huh?" he asked.

"Dusted out," Cotton answered, following him inside for the maps.

The attendant shook his head doubtfully. "Sure hope you make it. But just women and kids, in that heap—I don't know—"

"We'll make it," Cotton retorted. "They—they've got me!" He looked outside and saw the others waiting. "We'll make it," he said again, mostly to himself. He hurried to the car.

As Cotton started to get into the car beside Grandma, he felt an overwhelming urge to look back down the road. He whirled. Heat waves shimmered over the dusty road. Far back of them a bluish speck seemed to appear. Cotton's heart leaped. Was it Shag? He blinked and looked again, straining to see. There was no spot. Mirage. Must be, he thought. He climbed into the car, swallowing hard.

It didn't take long to cover the rest of western Kansas and reach the Colorado border. Cotton had looked forward to the moment with excitement. But eastern Colorado didn't look much different from Kansas, he decided as they traveled. Even the towns they passed through, Cheyenne Wells, Kit Carson, and Aroya, didn't look much different from Willow Creek, back home.

The towns were small, with wide flat prairie stretching for miles in between. About the only moving thing he'd seen was a jackrabbit now and then, sailing in long leaps across the road.

Cotton dozed. When he finally woke up, he realized the car was stopping. Beside him, Grandma jerked and snorted as she, too, came awake.

"Time for dinner, sleepyheads," Mama laughed. Her finger tapped the windshield. "Look out there."

Cotton looked, but everything appeared dull and unchanged to him.

"I see some funny, pointy clouds 'way up ahead," Ivy announced.

The clouds did look different somehow, Cotton thought. He squinted his eyes for a better look. Goose bumps tickled along his arms. "Those aren't clouds," he gasped, "they're mountains!"

"The Rocky Mountains," Mama announced.

Grandma opened the door and climbed out. She bent low, shading her eyes, staring in the direction of the high, snowy peaks. "Might as well be clouds," she prophesied, "we'll never get over 'em."

Laughter followed the remark, but under it was a note of fear. Cotton shrugged off his own uneasy feelings. He climbed from the car and jiggled the stiffness from his legs before going back to the boat.

"Hurry with the food box," his mother called. Cotton looked over to where she walked with the others, stretching their limbs and chattering about the mountains, and nodded.

He untied the ropes and lifted the food box from

the boat. Suddenly, an eerie feeling shook him from head to toe. He turned quickly and looked back down the road eastward. An empty ribbon of concrete stretched for miles back across the prairie.

"Son, bring the food," Mama said again. She came to his side. "What are you looking at?" she asked.

"I-I keep having this crazy feeling," he said, looking hard at the highway behind them. "I think Shag is back there, Mama. Trying to follow us."

Mama stared at him in astonishment. "That's silly, Cotton," she said finally. "We've come more than a hundred miles. Shag wouldn't, couldn't follow us that far. You're having a 'feeling' like you said. That's all it is. Shag is probably with Joe right now."

Grandma came stamping toward them. "Are we going to eat, or shall we just stand all day in this heat and gape?"

Slowly, as though coming out of a dream, Cotton handed Mama the food box. He got the water jug and dipper from the boat. What was wrong with him? If he kept up this fussing about Shag, they might never get to Oregon.

The midday sun beat down on them as they ate and drank, seated on the running boards of the Chevy. The meal was soon finished. Everyone washed and took a last drink from the water jug. Cotton made a mental note that it was almost empty. He'd fill it when they stopped next, probably in Denver. For the first time since April, Cotton and the other children put on shoes and stockings. The mountains ahead looked cold. Sweaters were unpacked and made handy.

It was time to go. Cotton started to climb into the car beside Grandma, then stopped. Had he heard a dog barking? He jerked back. He had heard a dog. He was sure. "I heard a dog bark, far off," he said aloud. "It's Shag."

"What kind of foolish notion is that?" Grandma snorted.

Cotton pulled away as Mama reached for him. His ears were filled with the far-off barking sound. Didn't the others hear it? He ran a short distance back down the road, ignoring the shouts that followed him. "See, something is coming up the road." Cotton pointed. "It's Shag, I know his bark."

The others joined him in the roadway. "You're acting plain stupid, Cotton," Ivy said, hands on her hips.

The dark spot grew larger and larger as they watched. Then came the sound of a motor. Ivy covered her mouth and began to giggle hysterically. "It's a truck, a green pickup. Cotton thought a pickup was a dog." Bent double under an attack of giggles, she stumbled back to the car, followed by Grandma, Mama, Daisy, and the little boys. "Beware the barking truck," Ivy choked out amid gasps of laughter.

Cotton scarcely heard her, so intent was he on the approaching truck.

"Cotton, come get in the car," Mama ordered sternly.

Cotton couldn't obey. It was as though his feet were rooted to the roadway. He stepped back, finally, as the shiny green pickup neared. As the flash of green roared by, Cotton read a blur of black words painted on the pickup door, HIDDEN VALLEY SHEEP RANCH.

Almost in the same instant, he saw the dog in the back of the pickup. And the blue and white Australian shepherd saw him. The dog hurled itself at him, against the wooden rails that held it prisoner. Its frenzied bark tore into Cotton's heart. Cotton's fists doubled up. "Shag," he screamed, "Shag, come back!"

He ran after the pickup, his legs churning with all the power he possessed. "Stop!" he shouted, "stop!" Shag's frantic barking grew fainter and fainter. It was no use.

His chest throbbed painfully as he trudged back to the car. Mama stood holding the door, her blue eyes puzzled, her face pink with anger.

"Cotton," she declared, "that wasn't Shag. It couldn't have been. The dog only looked like him. Do you realize we could be ten miles down the road by now?"

"S-sorry, Mama," Cotton panted, getting into the car. How Shag came to be in the pickup, he didn't know. But he had seen Shag just now, whether the others believed it or not. And he was going to keep on watching for that shiny green pickup with HIDDEN VALLEY SHEEP RANCH painted on the door.

Chapter 5
A Foolish Notion Comes True

At the; foot of the mountains, they came to Denver. Cotton tried to focus his attention on the excitement around him, but the thought of Shag weighed down his heart, as all around him horns honked like angry geese, whistles tooted, sirens screamed. They stopped for gasoline, but Cotton, in a cloud of gloom, remained in the car.

After Denver, the front range of the Rockies rose majestically. The highway curled and twisted higher and higher into the mountains like a thin, treacherous snake. Above them, snowy peaks were dazzling in the sun. On the right, the highway fell away into gorges so deep Cotton couldn't see the bottom, no matter how hard he tried. When he looked back over his shoulder, he was shocked to see clouds in the canyons below.

"Keep watch on the trailer, Cotton," Mama said in a harried voice. "We don't want to lose it going up these steep mountains."

"All right," he said. The back seat could have been

empty, there was so little sound coming from there. Cotton looked. The little boys, their bodies cramped and tangled, slept. The girls huddled together, away from the windows, wide awake. He grinned to show he wasn't afraid. They seemed to relax a little. He saw pink in Daisy's cheeks, a brightness in her blue eyes. A glad feeling rose in his throat.

"The mountains're good for something," he broke the silence. "Daisy looks like she's getting better already."

He turned just in time to see a green coupe come hurtling straight toward them around a curve. He froze. Mama turned the steering wheel deftly. They came very close to the snowy bank of the mountain-side. Cotton looked back, expecting to see the coupe go hurtling off the road into space. But it careened on its way, the outside wheels of the car just barely staying on the rim of the mountain, so it seemed to him. Cotton gulped and shook his head.

Grandma sat stiff and speechless beside him. Her thin fingers gripped his knee. If it made her feel better to hang on to him, that was all right. He sat up straighter in the seat as they continued higher and higher into the mountains. This part of going to Oregon wasn't dull—it was dangerous. And this kind of excitement he didn't like.

As though his thoughts were prophesying more trouble to come, the car jerked suddenly, coughed, and almost stopped. "Mama, what's the matter?" Cotton asked. A warning struck in his mind like a gong. Car trouble, their first clay? He'd been pretty dumb, thinking he could fix anything. How much did he know about a car?

"The engine seems to be getting hot," Mama said in a thin voice. "We've been climbing the last two hours, and the trailer makes it pull harder."

Cotton saw steam puff up from around the winged lady on the radiator cap. He drew in his breath. The car made a choking sound, slowed, and almost stopped. "I'll park and let the motor cool," Mama said as she pulled out by the side of the road.

"No wonder the car's hot," Cotton said when everyone had climbed from the car. He pointed to a sign by the roadside. It read, BERTHOUD PASS, Elevation 11,314 feet. "We're really high up," he said. "Cool, too." He buttoned his sweater.

Mama sat down on the running board of the car. "We'll fill the radiator in a little while, after it has a chance to cool." Grandma dropped down beside her.

Cotton grinned as he hurried to where the younger children scuffled happily in the snow. Snow, in the middle of summer! He scooped up a double handful of the wet fluff and hardened it into a ball with his palm, his fingertips tingling with cold. At that instant, he remembered his mother's words, "We'll fill the radiator." His grin faded and his heart thumped. There was no water in the jug, he had been planning to fill it in Denver. But when they stopped at the service station, he had stayed in the car.

Now what? If he hadn't been so worried about Shag he'd have remembered to fill the jug. He chewed his lip and glanced toward where Grandma and Mama sat. Both of them leaned back against the car, eyes closed, their faces peaceful in the sunshine. He wasn't going to worry them about it.

Cotton kicked angrily at the snow, then an idea came to him. He laughed. He examined the snowball in his hand. Snow was water. He'd put snow in the radiator! If he hurried, he could get it done while Mama and Grandma dozed. They wouldn't even know how dumb he'd been. Cotton tossed away the snowball, hitched up his overalls, and went to get the water dipper from the food box. He'd use it to dip the snow.

A moment later he put the dipper down on the front bumper, seized the winged lady with both hands, and turned. A dangerous hissing sound warned him, but it was too late. As the radiator cap loosened, a giant explosion burst in his face. He gave the cap a hard twist, screwing it down. He fell back then, blinded by the hot steam that had struck him before he could replace the cap. His own sharp cry of pain rang in his ears.

The side of his face, shoulder, and chest felt like they were on fire. He should have known better. Why didn't he remember the radiator had to cool? He stumbled in circles, hurting badly.

Mama was at his side in seconds. "Oh, Cotton, you shouldn't have taken the radiator cap off yet!" she echoed his thoughts. Afraid to open his eyes, Cotton let her lead him.

She pushed him down onto the running board. "It doesn't look too bad," she murmured, examining his burns. I suppose we should get some medicine as soon as we come to a town, though. Might get pretty painful otherwise."

Panic seized Cotton. There was no extra money for medicine. "It doesn't hurt hardly at all," he fibbed. "I don't need any medicine." He wasn't at all sure, though. His eyelids felt like hot ashes. Fearfully, he blinked them. Would he—could he—? Yes, he could see!

He looked up at Grandma standing over him, scrutinizing him, her face as pinched as a prune. Grandma! She was the answer. "You can fix this old burn, can't you?" Cotton asked.

A look of satisfaction at having a job to do warmed Grandma's stern countenance. She bustled importantly to the boat. "Lard," she said over her shoulder. "Lard, and keep it clean. Nothing better for burns."

Cotton turned to his mother. "I was trying to fill the radiator with snow, when—"

Grandma returned and motioned for him to be quiet. Her experienced fingers gently wiped the grease over his burning flesh. "Poor urchin," she clucked. "Your Papa expects you to fill his boots and you're not even half-growed. Folks expect too much of old ladies and young'uns. I've a mind to put a stop to this 'Oregon foolishness' yet!"

"Now, Grandma," Cotton jumped to his feet, "don't talk like that." They'd hardly gotten started! He gently brushed her busy hands away. "Everything's fine. There wasn't really anything wrong with the car. I can't feel this old burn," he said. "Your doctoring really fixed it, Grandma." Anything could happen if

Grandma started talking about turning back. Anything.

Time ticked slowly by. Finally, the hood of the Chevy was cool. Cotton's hand shook as he removed the radiator cap a second time. Nothing happened. The radiator was still warm enough, however, to turn the snow into water as he packed it in. A short time later his mother sat behind the wheel, the car motor chugging heartily.

"Everything's all right," Cotton called. "C'mon, everybody, get in the car."

Mama shook her head, frowning. "No," she said, "let's fix supper here, and spend the night. I'm afraid to drive along these curves in the dark. It's too dangerous. We'll get a fresh start in the morning."

Cotton looked around him at the high, lonely peaks, barely visible now in the descending darkness. In the last hour the air had turned stone-cold. Cotton remembered the speeding car that had almost hit them head-on and was glad Mama wanted to stay.

"I'll build a campfire," he nodded. As he worked he thought of Shag. Where was the pickup taking him? Would he ever see Shag again?

Next morning the motor purred, the heater thrummed a comfortable warmth into the interior of the car. The Baldwins hungrily devoured a breakfast of canned peaches and bread and butter.

"Going to be a good day," Cotton prophesied. "Like Grandpa used to say, 'I feel it in my bones.' "

Grandma snorted derisively. "May the Almighty

agree with you," she sniffed. "More than likely we'll never get off this mountain."

But she was wrong. They crossed the Colorado border into Utah. After a time the scene outside the car windows changed. Although high mountain peaks still circled them, the country they passed through was flat and desert-like.

His steam burns hurt, but Cotton paid little attention to them. He sat forward on the seat as they traveled, carefully watching for some sign of the green pickup and Shag.

They approached a small town, and he looked ahead for a sign that would tell him its name. Suddenly, as though created out of his own hopes, he saw something else. His heart began to bump wildly. For a minute he couldn't speak. Then he was yelling. "There it is!"

Up ahead, pulling out of that service station. The green pickup. The same green pickup!"

"Sit back," Mama ordered. "Stop waving your arms. Honestly, Cotton, I don't know what's the matter with you."

"It's the pickup," his voice thinned and almost failed. "But where's Shag? I can't see him!"

Everyone began talking at once. Mama ordered silence. "Cotton, I know how you feel about Shag," she said firmly, "but you're going to have to stop behaving so foolishly. Can't you realize, once and for all, that Shag is miles behind us in Kansas?"

"He's touched in the head," Grandma mumbled. "Leaving Kansas did that to him. Like I keep saying, the Baldwins should have stayed put where they were."

Why wouldn't they understand? Carefully, Cotton picked the words he wanted to say. "I know it sounds crazy," he admitted finally. "I know I hadn't ought to expect to see Shag this far from Kansas. But I ought to know my own dog—I've had 'im since he was a squirmy pup—right with me, every day. If we saw Dad all of a sudden, even though he's not supposed to be anywhere around here, wouldn't all of you know him?"

Cotton could feel Mama studying his face in amazement. He could tell she felt sorry for him, too. "People see such things because they want to see them more than anything else in the world," she said quietly. "It's a trick the imagination plays on the heart. You've got to get over this, Cotton, or you'll be seeing Shag everywhere you go, the rest of your life."

Mama was trying to help, he knew. But what had happened to Shag? He watched the green pickup fade out of sight. His heart yearned after it. "I won't mention him again, Mama," Cotton promised in an empty voice. He should have felt better, but he was stabbed with the thought that he had just let down one of the greatest friends he'd ever had.

Some time later, Cotton saw something stretched across the road before them. They approached it, and he saw the white, bubbling backs of hundreds of baaing sheep. Cotton's mind instantly cleared. His heart began to thump crazily. The green pickup— HIDDEN VALLEY SHEEP RANCH written on the door-now sheep! He said nothing. He'd promised. He bit his lip.

They stopped, waiting for the flock to part and let them through. Cotton sharply scanned the scene. There was no pickup in sight. Up on the hill to the left, though, he could see a man. A man, and yes, a dog. Cotton's mind buzzed so with excitement he felt the top of his head might come off. The dog was acting confused. The man was waving his arms, obviously trying to direct the dog to go after some stragglers that were disappearing into the brush further up the hill. In spite of himself, Cotton spoke aloud. "Shag never, never saw a sheep in his life." The man raised a stick. Cotton gasped and looked quickly at his mother.

Mama had seen it, too. "Go see," she said quickly, jumping from the car, "it does look like Shag."

Cotton sped up the hill, his heart roaring in his ears. Halfway up the hill, the dog saw him. It came rushing at him, barking in gleeful recognition.

"Shag," Cotton cried, half-laughing, half-crying. "Oh, Shag, boy." They collided, Shag's paws on Cotton's chest, Cotton's arms around the dog. They went down in a rolling heap. Cotton felt his wet cheeks being licked by a cool tongue. "Cut it out, you old dog," he laughed, rubbing the dog's coat lovingly, "that's enough, boy." Suddenly, Cotton was aware of two overalled legs standing over him.

Cotton threw himself across Shag's body. "Don't you touch him," he said, glaring at the stick in the man's hand, "don't you dare." Cotton looked up into a pair of kindly blue eyes and realized instantly that he had misjudged the man, and he was ashamed.

For a second the blue eyes twinkled. "I don't hit animals, never. This here's my directing stick. That's all I use it for. I will admit that dog has me up a tree, though."

"Shag's a good dog. He just never saw a sheep before," Cotton defended him. "It wouldn't take him long to learn though; he's smart. But wait, where'd you get him? Shag's my dog."

"Yeah," the sheepherder nodded, "I can see that. But how in tarnation—" he broke off and turned to watch Cotton's family streaming up the hill. " 'Lo, ladies," he said, tipping his battered hat to Grandma and Mama.

"It is Shag!" Mama shook her head in disbelief. She turned a struggling Kurt loose to toddle to the dog. The other children fell down beside Cotton, caressing Shag.

Cotton hid a grin as Grandma stooped stiffly to peer at Shag, both hands on her knees. "I declare," she exclaimed, "either I'm still in Kansas or that dog's sprouted wings and we're both in Utah!"

"Kansas, huh?" The sheepherder clapped a hand to his forehead. "Now things are beginning to make a little sense. I found that dog on the Kansas border, yesterday. He was by the road, looked dead as a door-nail laying there. When I stopped, though, I saw he was plumb worn out, that's all. There wasn't a house for fifty miles, so I fixed him up with water and eats and brought him along with me. Figuring to make a sheepdog of him."

"He was trying to follow us," Cotton said proudly. "I knew he was. You passed us in a green pickup. I knew Shag wouldn't want to be left behind." Cotton's chin began to quiver, silly-like, so he buried his face in Shag's coat.

For the next few moments Cotton paid little attention to the friendly conversation going back and forth above him. He was conscious only of the swells of gladness that kept rising in his chest like waves of wheat blowing in a prairie wind. He had Shag. Never again would they be parted. A sudden thought struck him and he sat up quickly.

"You—you won't try to keep us from taking him?" he asked the sheepherder.

The thin face crinkled into a wide grin. "Like I was telling your mama, just now, I never interfere with miracles. No, sir, that's another thing I never do."

Cotton felt more ashamed than ever. He stood up. "Thanks a lot, Mister." He reached for the sheepherder's hand and pumped it. "If it hadn't been for you picking him up and bringing him along, I wouldn't have Shag at all. And Shag is—well, he's— he's my dog."

While the others piled back into the car, Cotton rummaged in the boat for the clothes box. He drew out his Sunday, just-below-the-knee trousers. "Knickerbockers" Mama called them. With some quick juggling of their gear, he once again managed a cozy nest for

Shag in the prow of the boat. He lifted the dog into it, sneaking a glance at Mama, hoping she wouldn't notice. She did though. She made a face at him, but nodded her head in agreement, anyway. Shag turned around three times, flopped down on the trousers and sighed happily.

"Glad you like 'em," Cotton said. "I never did. Now, old clog, let's get on to Oregon." Cotton gave his mother a huge grin as he climbed into the car. "Ready," he said.

Chapter 6
Fire in the Night

Friday passed without incident and, at dusk, the Baldwins left Utah behind and entered Idaho's southern mountain region, a part of the Middle Rockies. There had been almost no houses for quite a while. During the past hour Cotton had seen one sheep camp nestled high on a wooded hillside, and several miles before that he had noticed a log cabin with a "Fire Warden" sign over the door. Mostly, the mountains looked lonely and forgotten.

"Campsite ahead," Cotton said. He motioned toward a tiny cut in the timber on top of the next hill.

He hadn't realized until now how tired and hungry he was. When they reached the spot, he added, "There's a little 'bridge ahead, down there at the bottom of the hill. Looks like a river. We'll have plenty of water."

"Glad you saw it, Cotton." Mama sighed, slowing the car. "Heaven knows we all could stand a good cleaning up." She stopped the car. "Let's see now," she went on, looking around, "since the shoulder of the road is too narrow to park on, I think it will be best to back in, and park between those two big rocks."

"I'll direct," Cotton said, "if you'll let me get out."

The whole family looked like funny wooden puppets, Cotton thought, as they set up camp. But no wonder. Riding in a car day after day made everybody stiff.

Supper seemed to give them all new life. The sizzling fried potatoes and creamed corn sure were good. Cotton began to wonder if he'd have room for the canned purple plums Mama had promised for dessert. When the time came, he found he needn't have worried.

After the others had turned in, Cotton sat on his quilt by the fire, Shag curled beside him. The moon was a silver ball over the tops of the trees. He felt clean and happy down to his toes. When the dishes were washed and packed in the food box, they had all taken "sponge baths," as Grandma called them.

"Makes a body feel fresh as a new-hatched chick, soap and water does," she had said. Cotton agreed.

As he sat caressing Shag's warm coat, thoughts of the Pawnee bow crowded into his mind. He trembled a second, then relaxed. They had made it this far, hadn't they? Getting Shag back was a sign their bad luck was over. There wasn't anything to worry about. They wouldn't need the bow and quiver money.

"Don't forget to turn out the lantern before you go to bed, Son," his mother's drowsy voice broke into his thoughts.

"I won't, Mama," Cotton said softly. " 'Night, Mama." He glanced up at the lantern that sat on top of the canvas-covered load in the boat. It shed a big circle of light over them—Daisy, Ivy, and the little boys making up the smaller rolls between Mama and Grandma in their blankets. He sighed. Taking care of them sure enough was a man-size job.

He turned back to gaze into the crackling flames of the campfire. Sometimes it was hard to believe they were actually on their way, but they were—and when they got to Oregon—He'd climb mountains, every last one he could get to. He'd explore, and fish, and hunt. 'Course, he'd spend some time at the farm, too. Somebody had to help with the peach growing.

He lost his train of thought as a vision of a ripe, golden peach hung before his eyes, dripping sweet juice. He licked his lips and dreamily closed his eyes. Hardly realizing what he was doing, Cotton snuggled back onto his quilt and fell asleep.

Later, Cotton sat up with a start, breathing hard, his chest clamped with sweat. He'd been having a dream. A terrible dream where snarling, shrieking animals breathed fire and smoke. Cotton shook his head to clear it. Suddenly, horror ran through him like ice water. The ghastly noises, the smoke stinging his nose and eyes weren't a dream. They were real!

His whole body shook as he lurched to his feet. The boat! Orange, foot-high flames ate gluttonously at the canvas cover. He saw the lantern on its side, kerosene spreading a dangerously wide circle over the tarp.

"Mama!" Cotton said. "Fire! Wake up, everybody!"

He lunged toward the boat, aware too late of the commotion at his feet. He was falling. Shag, entangled in a snarling battle with a strange small animal, rolled away from his legs. He landed with a thud.

Cotton sprang to his feet, grabbed his quilt, swinging it up and over down on the flames again and again.

But the quilt only seemed to fan the flames. The blaze flared up more viciously than ever, its loud crackling filled him with panic. "Get up!" he yelled hoarsely. "Wake up! Somebody help!"

Voices cried out behind him as he tried to smother the flames with the quilt. His stomach knotted as the flames grew and licked painfully at his face. It was useless, the fire had too much of a start on him.

He had to think of another way to stop it, quick. He made for the hitch where the boat trailer joined the car. Smoke swirled thickly around him, robbing his breath and leaving him choking for air. He fumbled frantically to locate the hitch. If only he could get the boat away from the car, away from everything—

A glad sob tore his throat as the coupling pin came free. Cotton grabbed the iron trailer tongue and lifted. The muscles in his arms stung painfully from the effort but he held on. Slowly, he pushed the blazing boat back away from the car, toward the river. Even with his full strength thrown against it, he could see he was moving the boat only inches at a time. It would take forever! He didn't have time!

Sweat poured down his face. His skin felt like it was on fire.

Suddenly, some of the weight lifted from his arms. The trailer picked up speed, moving much easier.

The clearing sloped in this spot down toward the river—that was it! Maybe—a chance, Cotton thought, relief flooding through him. The boat moved effortlessly now. But he had to hold the tongue up. If he let go, the tongue would drop, stopping the trailer.

He stumbled into a run, trying to keep up with the trailer as it rolled faster and faster down the hill. Panting for breath, he held the boat on as straight a course as possible. Another few yards and it would all be over. Suddenly, he felt his toe hit hard against a rock, twisting his foot sharply sideways. It was as though a thousand small knives were plunged into his left ankle. A scream rang in his ears and Cotton realized in pain and despair that it was his own. He fell to his knees, tried once to regain his feet, but it was as though the twisted ankle made his leg useless. He felt the trailer tongue being ripped by gravity from his fingers.

Cotton looked up from where he'd fallen. The trailer careened down the hill, the boat a solid mass of flames. The iron tongue suddenly dropped, the trailer zigzagged wildly. "No!" Cotton cried hoarsely. The inferno came to a stop a few feet from the trunk of a giant fir tree. If the tree caught, the entire forest would go up in flames.

Struggling against the pain that burned in his ankle, Cotton lunged to his feet. He staggered toward the trailer, his left foot dragging. The trailer was so close to the edge of the river bank—if only he could reach it in time, push it over the edge. Throwing his left arm up to protect his face, Cotton hobbled in, reached down for the trailer tongue. He whirled back with a sharp cry as the heat of the flames stung his skin as if it were fire itself. He couldn't do it —if he tried again he'd be burning, too. But he had to get the boat into the river, away from the trees. There was no other way to end this awful thing.

Maybe, if he were wet all over—On one leg, Cotton hopped down the incline to the river's edge. He gulped once, pinched his nose between thumb and forefinger, and threw himself into the river. The water closed in over his head, surrounding him like a cold, black shroud. He flailed his arms and good leg, driving himself upward. He gasped for air as his head cleared water. He dog-paddled to the bank and crawled out, dragging his useless foot.

Cotton clambered up the incline. He hopped to the burning boat and grabbed up the trailer tongue. With every fiber of his body, he shoved. Flames licked at him, but he ignored them. He gathered his muscles for another mighty push, then the trailer tongue wrenched from his fingers as the boat went over the edge.

His whole body shook. Cotton stood watching the circles of flame that were the tires carrying the boat into the river. The burning boat sizzled and spat in the water like a giant monster.

Had it all happened in minutes? It seemed like a nightmare that had lasted for hours. Cotton felt weak and empty as he turned. Through the darkness he could see the figures beating at the flames that licked at the bark of the big fir. "Smother it, Mama," he yelled as he approached. "Beating only makes it worse."

Like the Statue of Liberty, Daisy stood frozen, holding the coffee pot aloft. Cotton took it from her, tossed the lid aside, and dashed the remains on the fire. He dropped to his knees and scooped a pot full of soft earth and passed it to her. "Throw it on the fire," he ordered. He repeated the performance until the last tiny flame flickered out.

Minutes ticked by. No one moved or made a sound. "I'm sorry," Cotton finally choked out through parched lips. "I forgot to turn the lantern out. It's my fault we lost the boat and everything."

"It's all right," Mama murmured, hugging him to her side. "It's all right now. We owe our thanks to you and God, that a burning forest didn't come down on our heads."

Grandma let out a breath that was more a hiss than a sigh. She shook her head and whirled back toward the car.

Cotton followed the others through the moonlit night to the campsite, numb with despair over the loss of the boat and their belongings with it.

Daisy came up close beside him. "You all right, Cotton?" she asked in a small voice. "You didn't get hurt or anything, did you?"

Cotton nodded, ignoring the quivering that still

went on in his stomach and his pain-wracked ankle. "I'm all right, Daisy."

They gathered close together by the campfire. Ivy began to wail. "We're never going to get to Oregon," she sobbed. "I just know it. All our stuff's burned up, it's just trouble, trouble, all the way."

Cotton suddenly came to life. He whirled, grabbed Ivy by the shoulders and shook her. "We are so going to make it. Don't say we aren't. We've still got the car. We've got our food box and our blankets. We're not naked, are we?" Ivy's head bobbed back and forth until it seemed it would fly off. Cotton let his hands drop, for he realized suddenly it was himself he was angry at, not Ivy. "Gosh, Ivy, I'm sorry," he apologized. "I know everything's a mess, mostly on my account, but don't say we won't get to Oregon. Because we have to, and we will."

She turned away from him, sobbing mournfully. Cotton couldn't help feeling sorry for her, and ashamed of himself, as she crawled into her blankets like a sad little kitten.

Something wet touched the back of Cotton's hand. He looked down. "Sh-Shag, you—you trouble-maker!" he sputtered. Shag tipped his head to one side in a bewildered fashion. Cotton was instantly sorry. "There I go, yelling at you, too." He patted the bony head. "What'd you tie into, anyway, a weasel? Guess he's the one that tipped over the lantern and started the fire. That's probably when you lit into him. Good boy, Shag," he said, "you're a good old dog."

Mama said wearily, "Come, turn in, Cotton. There's nothing more we can do tonight."

But Cotton couldn't sleep. Pain shot through his ankle each time he moved. He lay motionless, staring wide-eyed into the darkness, trying to ignore his throbbing ankle. Twice he got up and hobbled through the moonlight to the big fir tree, Shag trotting protectively behind him. He wanted to be sure the tree didn't start burning again.

Cotton awoke the next morning trying to convince himself he hadn't heard the rusty hinge sound of a rooster crowing. Then it came again. A rooster? Way out here in the mountains, away from everything? Cotton grinned, the crowing sounded so good, so country-familiar.

He lay awake, listening, hating to leave his warm bed. After a moment he threw back his quilt and got shakily to his feet. He winced—the ankle hurt. He hobbled toward the cold gray ashes of last night's campfire. He'd start the fire, maybe even fix breakfast —sort of make up for the trouble he'd caused.

A sharp gasp sounded behind him. It was Mama. "Son, you're hurt!" She got up and came toward him.

Cotton dropped down by the pile of sticks he'd gathered the night before and began to arrange them in the ashes. He grinned up at Mama. "Just my ankle."

"Your ankle—why, look at you. Your face is red in spots, and black in other places, and you haven't an eyelash left to your name!"

Cotton shrugged and began to explore his face with his fingers.

"Look at your ankle, it's twice its normal size," Mama continued to scold. "Why didn't you tell me last night?"

"I caused enough trouble, Mama," he answered quietly. He struck a match to the kindling. The fire caught, held, then began to crackle merrily. "What are you doing?" he asked Mama as she removed a dishtowel from the food box and began tearing it into strips.

"Binding that ankle," she said. "Sit still."

"That does feel better," Cotton said a short time later. He touched the bandaged ankle gingerly. "Now what?" he demanded and drew back as she began to wash his face.

"You're still not too old to have your Mama wash your face," she said, smiling. "Now sit still, like you were told."

He didn't really mind. In fact, he felt all shivery-warm inside from the gentle attention. Still, he wouldn't want the others to wake up and catch him getting his face washed like a baby. "That's enough," he said quickly as Ivy stirred. "Family's going to want breakfast."

With the boat gone, it was necessary to find a place to carry the food box, bedding, and Shag. Cotton decided to put the food box on top of the car and the bedding on top of that. He tore a worn blanket into strips to make a rope. By fastening the blanket rope back and forth several times from the winged lady in front and the bumper in back, Cotton was able to tie on the baggage more or less securely.

"We sure look junky," Ivy said disgustedly.

"You haven't seen anything yet," Cotton retorted. "Shag's going to ride in your lap the rest of the way to Oregon, Miss Smarty."

"M-m-mama-a-a," Ivy wailed.

"Hush," Mama smiled. "Cotton's teasing. But Shag will have to go in back with you younger ones. We'll keep the baby in the front seat with us."

At last they were ready to go. To Cotton it seemed strange, starting out without the boat and trailer behind them, but they could travel faster now, without the trailer to pull. They'd be with Dad sooner.

It wasn't fair, though, that Mama and Grandma had lost almost the last of their things in the fire. On his account, too. For an instant, he almost wished there were no bow and quiver under the back seat.

Chapter 7
Snake River Danger

They had traveled about a mile. "Look, a fire warden's cabin!" Cotton pointed to a cluster of small green buildings nestled against a backdrop of tall timber. "I think we should stop," he said. "I can tell him about the big tree. I've read that a tree like that can burn for days on the inside, without anybody realizing it. He could keep watch."

Mama nodded and stopped the car.

Cotton hobbled up to the neat little fence that surrounded the cabin. Over the cabin door hung a sign, IDAHO STATE FORESTRY DEPARTMENT. From somewhere behind the building, a rooster crowed.

Cotton relaxed. The one he'd heard earlier, probably. Shouldn't be too hard to talk to a forest ranger who kept chickens, he decided.

A slender man in woodsman's garb answered Cotton's knock. Cotton looked up into a bronze face with brown eyes that were smiling.

"I want to report a fire," Cotton said. "Last night this weasel, or some other kind of animal, got into our camp and knocked over our lantern. But it was my fault—"

The warden listened attentively to the whole story, his face grave. "Glad you reported it, son. Too many people don't," he said.

On they traveled, through Burley, Twin Falls, and Buhl. It was a pleasurable morning, except for the baby, who, restless and fussy as a caged wild bear cub, jerked too many locks of hair and twisted too many noses.

At noon they stopped before a run-down little store squatting alone on a bluff above the Snake river. Two black-haired, copper-skinned men lounged against the porch pillars.

"Those men sure look different," Ivy spoke up. "Black cowboy hats, cowboy shirts and blue jeans, but beaded belts and moccasins. Which are they supposed to be, cowboys or Indians?"

"Indian cowboys, no doubt," Mama said quietly. "And you children mind your manners."

"It's the river I'm interested in," Cotton said, climbing from the car. Shag was already ahead of him, nosing along the bank. Cotton looked down into the swirling depths and automatically stepped back. Anyone who ever fell in there, he decided, would never get out alive.

Behind him, Mama was giving orders. "Ivy, play with the baby outside while Grandma and Daisy help me buy what we need. Bobby, you come along, too."

She hugged Kurt. "Poor little tyke, you're so tired of being penned up in the car. Cotton, you'd better check the tires. The left rear tire is low."

Cotton nodded, came back from the river's edge, and pulled out the front seat to get the tire pump. He set it on the ground and pushed the seat back in place. He gave the river another glance, shook his head, and went on with the job.

He screwed the pump hose to the tire valve and drew the pump handle up and pushed it down again and again—methodically pumping air into the tire. His thoughts returned to the Snake- What a river like that could do for Kansas! It'd make it another Rainbow Valley, probably. They wouldn't be calling Kansas the "Dust Bowl," anyhow.

When he had finished, Cotton slumped down on the running board to wait. Some time later he felt his arm being jiggled frantically. He turned and saw Ivy's white face. Her eyes were wide with fear—her lips moved silently.

"For corn sakes, what's the matter?" he demanded. Ivy's mouth continued to open and close like a fish out of water.

"I-I-I lost K-K-Kurt," Ivy stammered at last. "I lost the baby."

It didn't make sense. "What do you mean, you lost Kurt?" Cotton demanded, jumping to his feet. Shag circled them, whimpering.

Ivy's face crumpled. Tears filled her eyes. "I didn't mean to," she sobbed. "I crossed the road to get these blue flowers," she held up the dust-caked bouquet in her hand, "and when I came back Kurtie was gone. I looked and looked, Cotton. I can't find him anywhere."

"Aw, quit blubbering," Cotton said. "He's around here; he can hardly walk, where would he go?" Cotton circled the car. "Kurtie," he called. "Hey, Kurt, it's time to go. Come get in the car!" He held his breath and waited. There was no answer. Cotton's glance fastened on the river and his heart leaped into his throat.

"Go to the store and tell the others," Cotton ordered. "We'd better find him quick. Shag and I'll start looking."

"Find him for me, Cotton, please," Ivy begged as she ran.

Cotton hurried first to the Indians. "Have you seen a little kid, about this high, with white hair?" he asked, holding a hand out to show Kurt's height. "He was wearing a yellow sunsuit."

The Indians shrugged silently and shook their heads. Cotton studied the dark faces a moment, decided they were telling the truth, and whirled away.

With drumming heart, he went to the river and hobbled swiftly along the top of the bank. "Kurtie just couldn't have fallen in," Cotton whispered aloud to Shag. "He's probably hiding somewhere 'cause he doesn't want to get back into the car." Cotton's glance traveled frantically down along the steep river bank dotted with rocks and clumps of brush. "Kurt," he called, "where are you?" Overhead, a bird trilled mockingly, the breeze whispered in the tops of the trees.

Behind Cotton, the rest of the family had come out

of the store. He could hear them calling Kurt, sounding as scared as he felt.

Where could the little guy have gone? Was he behind a rock? A bush? Or—in the river? "Kurt," Cotton pleaded, looking swiftly about, "come out and let big brother give you a piggyback ride." Nothing happened.

A huge, flat boulder lay in Cotton's path. He hopped to the top, tottered and swayed a second, then froze like a statue. In the sand below was Kurt's limp yellow sunsuit. "Kurt, where are you?" Cotton yelled. There was no answer.

Back home in Kansas, when it was so sultry a person could hardly stand it, Kurt loved nothing better than having all his clothes off, with a pan of water to splash in. Had he seen the river, thought it would be fun to play in? Cotton turned sick all over. He bounded off the rock and plunged on. He had to find him. "Kurt!" he screamed.

All at once, above the noise of the blood pounding in his head, Cotton heard something from down over the edge of the bank. He skidded to a stop. Almost out of sight beside a clump of green leafy brush, about twenty feet below, sat Kurt's tiny white figure. The baby was struggling to get nearer the rushing water close below him, and at the same time he gripped a sickeningly thin branch of shrub.

Cotton opened his mouth and then closed it quickly.

If he yelled, if he scared Kurtie, the little guy might let go of the branch, and—

Suddenly, there was a noise behind Cotton as someone kicked a rock. He whirled. Ivy! He motioned frantically for her to remain still.

There was no time to lose. He took a deep breath and called down softly to the baby. "Don't move, Kurtie. Brother wants to come, too. Stay there and wait for Cotton."

The toddler's little moon face tipped up to look at him, his chubby body jiggled with excitement. "Watah," he gurgled happily.

Cotton swung down over the edge of the bank, his fingers and toes pawing for a hold on the steep rocky bank. He forced calmness into his voice, "Don't move, Kurtie. Wait right there for Cotton."

Cotton flattened himself against the bank, fighting gravity as it dragged at his whole body. He inched slowly downward. Suddenly, Cotton's foot slipped, each handhold gave way, and he was sliding down the bank so fast it was like a horrible nightmare of swift motion and stabbing rocks and sticks. Pain flared in his injured ankle. He grabbed desperately, felt a jutting rock and clung. The rock loosened under his hand, he set his jaw and held on.

He pulled himself into a half-sitting, half-lying position. He gasped for air and shook his head to clear the dust from his eyes. He looked down. Not an arms-length away, Kurt stared at him.

"Cotton ouchy?" the tot asked, his lips a sorrowful pout.

Cotton grinned shakily. "You bet I hurt, you little scamp." Cautiously he edged toward Kurt, grabbed his arm. "We're going up to see Ivy," he said, his voice quivering. "See Sissy up there?" Cotton nodded to where Ivy peered white-faced over the edge of the bank, Shag whimpering beside her.

Cotton clutched at the ground with one hand, held Kurt with the other, and inched upward. All at once, the baby's arm slipped from his grip. Cotton grabbed and missed as the baby began creeping away from him.

"No!!" Kurt grunted, the shake of his little round head stubborn. "Watah!"

"Kurtie," Cotton croaked, "come with me. Ivy will get you some water." He reached desperately for the baby. Kurt edged away.

Hearing new sounds above them, Cotton glanced up. Thankfully, he saw Mama, lying on her stomach with arms outstretched, waiting. Her eyes were dark with shock, her face white. Her lips were moving and Cotton knew she was praying. "Look," Cotton said, "look up at Mama. Mama wants to see us."

The toddler chortled happily at sight of Mama. "Mama," he squealed. Cotton could hardly believe his eyes as Kurt scrambled up the bank on his hands and feet, sure-footed as a little goat. Evidently, Kurt had had enough of trying to get to the river, and Mama always was a welcome sight to him. Cotton held his breath until the baby reached the top, then closed his eyes in relief as Mama grabbed Kurt by the arms and swung him up over the edge.

Eternities later, it seemed to Cotton, he reached the top himself. Ivy was at him at once, hugging and kissing him. "I knew it," she sobbed, "I knew you'd save Kurtie for me. I've been a bad sister, but you're the bravest, wonderfullest brother in the whole world!"

Cotton brushed her off feebly. "Quit it," he panted. "You don't have to slobber to thank me." He smiled to show he wasn't really angry. He looked to where his mother sat, hugging Kurt and rocking to and fro. Like Ivy's, her eyes also brimmed with tears. But she was laughing.

"George Cotton Baldwin," she said happily, "you saved your brother's life and you'll just have to take the kissing that goes with the thanks." In the next moment, she, too, was smothering him with kisses. Shag joined the hero worship with moist licks of his own.

Several minutes later they headed back to the car, picking up Kurt's sunsuit and dressing him on the way. Cotton walked tall beside Mama, hardly limping at all. He looked at Kurt, sleepily straddling her hip, and felt wonderful inside.

Daisy, pulling Bobby by the hand, came hurrying toward them. "You found him, oh, you found him," she cried joyfully. She threw her arms around Mama and Kurt. "I'm so glad," she said, "I was afraid—" Suddenly she gasped and straightened. "I almost forgot," she wrung her hands, "Grandma is fighting with an Indian!"

"What?" Cotton and his mother exclaimed together.

"Grandma's fighting with one of those Indian cowboys," Daisy repeated. "The other one rode off on a horse, earlier."

All of them broke into a run, but Cotton, hopping

on one leg, was first to the scene. In the dooryard of the ramshackle store, he saw Grandma shaking her fist at the Indian backed against a shaggy pinto pony.

"Grandma, what're you doing?" Cotton asked, shocked.

"I helped run you redskins out of Kansas territory years ago," Grandma screeched, and Cotton knew she hadn't heard him. "But it looks like you sprung up again out here," she went on. "I'm not of a mind to stay out West, if I'm going to have to start warring with Injuns again. Where's the white child?" she demanded. "You know you stole him. You took him for a white slave." The Indian threw up his hands, opened his mouth to speak, but Grandma lashed out at him again, "Imagine, stealing children in this day and age."

She was making an awful mistake. Cotton shouted, "Grandma—" but she cut him off.

"Stay out of this." She waved for him to remain behind her. "This savage has kidnapped your brother but I can make him talk."

"Grandma, listen!" Cotton pleaded, grabbing her arm, "I found Kurtie. He's all right." He turned her around so she could see the others hurrying toward them, Kurt drowsy in Mama's arms.

Grandma sagged against him, almost causing Cotton to lose his balance. "G-g-grandma?" he questioned anxiously, struggling to hold her up. "You all right?"

" 'Course I am," she said, suddenly standing bolt upright. She threw her shoulders back and took a deep breath. "No harm done," she said airily, "that heathen can't understand English, didn't know a word I was saying."

"Grandma," Cotton begged, "c'mon."

"Mam you're talking about the wrong century," the Indian broke in, speaking in perfect English.

Grandma jumped, clutching Cotton's arm until it hurt.

"I'm just a no-good, twentieth-century cowpoke," the Indian stated. "But my Granddaddy, that's a different story. He was the meanest Shoshone of them all. And if he was looking for a white slave, I think he'd rather have a pepper-pot Granny than a tow-headed papoose, any day."

Cotton could see the Indian was teasing, but Grandma looked as scared as Cotton had ever seen her. The Indian advanced toward her. Grandma backed up, almost knocking Cotton over. Suddenly, the Indian put his hand over his mouth and gave a war cry that would have been blood-curdling in any century.

"Oh!" Grandma shrieked, "Let's get out of here." Cotton jumped aside as she scurried toward the car. He wondered if she wasn't breaking a speed record, for grandmothers, anyway. He hobbled to catch up as she swiftly herded the others toward the car like a mother hen trying to protect her chicks from a marauding hawk.

"But I didn't get my groceries," Mama protested.

"Never mind," Grandma shrilled, "let's get away from here!"

Mama shrugged. "Maybe I can get them in the next town."

Cotton looked back as they pulled onto the highway. He wasn't surprised to see the Indian slapping his thigh and roaring with laughter.

"You never know what those devils will do," Grandma shook her head, "never could be sure."

"I don't think he would have hurt us," Daisy admonished. "Today Indians are no different from other people, except for their color."

"That's right," Cotton agreed. "Even in the old days, they weren't all bad. What about Chief Keola? He gave Grandpa the—the—" Cotton gulped. He hadn't mentioned the Pawnee bow since the day of the sale. "—the Pawnee bow," he finished quietly.

Chapter 8
Trouble by the Ton

"We've been four days on the road; how is our money holding out, Veri?" Cotton heard Grandma ask, late that afternoon when they stopped to stretch their legs.

That's what he'd like to know. He turned from where he'd been watching a prairie dog disappear into some rocks and looked at Mama.

"Bring my pocketbook from the car, please, Cotton," she said.

He got the handbag and gave it to her, moistening his lips as she examined the bills and coins inside. She closed her eyes and began figuring. It seemed a hundred hours passed before she opened her eyes and spoke.

"I don't think we have anything to worry about. If we're careful, we should have just enough to get us to Rainbow Valley and Pres. Not counting Cotton's money." Mama squeezed his arm. "Barring trouble,

Son, you'll still have your money when we get to Oregon."

Cotton tried to smile. So far, so good, he thought, and wiped the sweat from his forehead.

When they were moving again, Cotton felt better. He studied the map. Boise was only a few miles ahead. After that it was only about sixty-five miles to the Oregon border. Why, they were practically there! It'd sure feel good to let Dad take over.

At that instant he noticed the temperature gage. He sat up straight, startled. "Mama, look, I think the engine's getting hot!"

She looked and frowned. "We'd better find some water for the radiator, now. I don't want it getting overheated like it did before in Colorado. And if I remember right, we're again nearly out of water."

Cotton scanned their desert-like surroundings. "No sign of water, no creek or anything—" he said. They drove on. The temperature needle wavered dangerously toward the red H. Averting his worried glance, Cotton saw something else.

"There, Mama." He pointed. "Way up ahead. I can walk to that house and ask for some water."

He was ready when they stopped at the end of the lane leading to the dingy yellow house set back about a mile from the highway.

"I'll help too—if it's all right with Cotton," Ivy said.

Cotton nodded. "Sure." Soon, they were out of the car hurrying down the lane toward the house, Ivy carrying a fruit jar rummaged from the food box, Cotton toting the water jug.

The sun felt good on the back of Cotton's head. He looked up and saw a hawk circling gracefully against the bright blue sky. Such a beautiful, free thing. Cotton began to sing, "Home, home on the range—" The sound startled a young cottontail from under an old wagon beside the lane. He watched the rabbit hop away across the field. Cotton laughed and continued his song. Insects hummed in the sparse grass, adding their music to his. The lane to the house was turning out to be longer than it looked, but he didn't care. It felt good to be walking instead of riding for a change.

They weren't in Oregon yet, though. He quickened his steps. The house loomed larger and larger in front of them as they walked. Beside Cotton, Shag growled deep in his throat. The sound of warning caused the skin on Cotton's neck to prickle. "What's the matter, boy?" he asked.

"Looks like a haunted house to me," Ivy whispered, moving closer to Cotton.

Cotton studied the bare yard, the blank windows of the rickety, two-story house. "Nah," he shook his head, "it's just an old empty house, that's all. Nobody living here. There's a well over there, though." He headed toward the pump located a few feet to the right of the house, rusty red in the bright midday sun.

Shag pressed against Cotton's leg, his shoulders hunched, a low, ominous growl rumbling in his throat. Cotton reached down and caressed the shaggy head. "You think there's something in that old house, boy? Well, probably there is—rats, mice, or some little old desert animal. He won't hurt us though, fella, so quit worrying."

"I—I think it's something bad," Ivy insisted. "I've got scaredy shivers all over. Let's go back to the car, Cotton."

If that wasn't just like a girl. Cotton shook his head and continued toward the pump. "A lot of good it would do us to go back to the car without water. We're stuck right here until we get some water in the radiator. Besides, what could be in the house, a ghost? You know better than that."

That Ivy! Now she had his stomach feeling funny.

But he was going to get some water and that was that. Suddenly, something soft thudded against Cotton's back. His knees threatened to buckle, the water jug slipped from his fingers and clanked to the ground. He whirled, his heart beating furiously.

Ivy, her eyes wide, cringed behind him. Finally, she stammered, "I-I'm sorry. I-I thought if I closed my eyes I wouldn't—wouldn't be so scared, and I bumped into you."

"Ivy, don't be such a fraidy cat," he hissed. He picked up the jug, ashamed at how his hand shook. "Didn't I tell you we had to get some water? Then we'll get out of here." He spoke sternly: "If you bump into me again, Ivy, you'll wish it was a ghost after you, and not me!"

Cotton stepped up onto the board platform built around the pump. He grasped the pump handle. At the same instant, a thick, snuffling sound came from the direction of the house. Cotton froze. Behind him, Ivy gasped. Cotton listened but no other sound came.

"So," he whispered to Ivy, "maybe there is something in the house. Whatever it is, Shag is here to help us." He nodded to where the Australian shepherd trotted warily back and forth, eying the house. "We have to have water, though."

He drew the handle up and pushed it down. A loud squawk issued from the pump like the cry of an injured vulture. Sweat popped out all over Cotton's body, cooling his skin under his hot clothing. "Pump has to be primed," he mumbled.

Ivy crept nearer to him. He could see her shivering. "We'll be out of here quick," Cotton consoled her. "There's some water in the jug. I'll prime the pump with that." He unscrewed the cap from the jug and poured the water into the top of the pump. Gripping the handle firmly, he jerked it up and down as fast as he could. The pump made a choking sound, coughed, then water poured out. Cotton waited for the rusty water to clear, then held the jug under the spout until it was running over.

"Let's go," Ivy pleaded.

Cotton swiftly replaced the cap on the jug. "Give me the jar, first," he said. He filled it and gave it back. "Now, we're getting out of here." He grabbed Ivy's hand and tore out for the lane that led back to the highway.

Suddenly, an explosion of clanking metal and splintering wood burst behind them. Cotton's blood chilled. He whirled to look. Charging around the house came an enormous bull. Barn-red, with a white face, he looked to be as big as a boxcar. Cotton gulped as the bull skidded to a halt. A battered tin wash basin, pierced through by a wickedly curved horn, sat on the creature's head like a jaunty cap. As Cotton stood frozen, the bull's fiery red eyes seemed to bore into them.

The bull broke into a trot straight at them, then suddenly stopped. The bull would be charging them any second! Like a sleepwalker, Cotton moved backward, pushing Ivy with him. Unless they could jump out of his way, they didn't have a chance. Cotton tensed, prepared to lunge to the right or left, whichever direction would deliver them safely from the massive head and gleaming horns.

The bull raked the sunbaked earth ferociously, sending up small clouds of dust—and charged. Cotton saw a blur of blue and white hurl at the bull. Shag! Cotton whirled to run, pulling Ivy with him. Over his shoulder he saw the bull stop short, momentarily checked. Shag swiftly circled the animal, barking furiously and nipping at the bull's heels. The bull jerked around in a circle like a broken merry-go-round.

Suddenly, the gleaming horns swiped at Shag, and the dog swerved out of reach. "Shag," Cotton yelled, "c'mon. he'll kill you!" As he spoke, the massive head caught Shag in the side. It was like a horrible nightmare. Cotton saw Shag and the wash basin tossed skyward like two lifeless toys. A sob ripped from Cotton's throat. "Shag!" he screamed. "Shag!" He gave Ivy a shove. "Keep going and you won't get hurt," he cried in a thick voice. "I'm going back to get Shag."

He wrenched free as Ivy tried to stop him. "Cotton, don't go back! Don't!"

He ignored her. "Run! Take this water to the car. That bull isn't going to kill Shag!" His mind was clear. Shag's quiet form lay about ten feet from the rickety buckboard by the lane. If he was quick enough, he could run, pick up Shag, then duck under the wagon before the bull took another notion to plow into them.

"Tell Mama to bring the car!" he shouted after Ivy. She nodded, sobbing as she ran.

Cotton raced toward Shag's helpless body, praying fervently for enough time, his gaze riveted to the bull as he ran. The critter wasn't going to catch him off guard, no matter what. Cotton's heart thundered in his ears as he saw the sharp hoofs rip at the earth, the mammoth head weave and shake only inches from the ground. The bull was going to charge again! Shag's defenseless body was the target.

"Yieee!" Cotton screamed suddenly, "Leave him alone, hear?" He waved his arms like a windmill gone wild. The massive head jerked upward, the fiery red eyes stared. Cotton reached Shag, scooped the limp form into his arms, whirled back toward the wagon, and dove beneath it. "We made it, boy. You're going to be okay—you're just knocked out."

Looking up, a scream of horror caught and died in Cotton's throat. Like an onrushing locomotive, the bull was coming, head low, horns ready, dirt flying. Cotton couldn't move. The bull hit with the power of a tornado, the wagon tipped, and boards splintered, popping like rifle shots. The wagon went over as though it were no more than a matchbox. Suddenly exposed, Cotton hesitated. The bull backed away as though stunned. Cuddling Shag against him, Cotton leaped to his feet and whipped around to the back of the overturned wagon.

Seconds passed like hours. Then he heard the Chevy roaring up the lane, horn bugling. Tears of relief stung Cotton's eyes. He peeked around the corner of the wagon. Mama's face was set hard as granite as she drove the noisy Chevy straight at the bull. Cotton watched the bull trot a short distance away. It stared back quizzically at the odd contraption that had suddenly appeared on the scene. His mother backed the car toward the wagon, and Grandma flung her door open. Cotton held Shag and raced for it, throwing himself inside. He quickly slammed the door.

When they left the lane and turned onto the road, Cotton found his voice. "Whew," he said weakly, "that was too close for comfort. I thought sure that bull was going to smash us to smithereens. Poor Shag just acts like he's dead but he's still breathing."

"Look," Daisy said.

Cotton looked back to where she pointed. Two figures on horseback had appeared and were bearing down on the bull.

"The bull must have gotten away from somebody," Ivy said faintly, "and decided to go house haunting."

Mama stopped the car by the side of the road. She

leaned back in the seat. She looked very strange. "Are you sick, Mama?" Cotton asked.

She shook her head. "I honestly don't know if my nerves are going to hold up until we reach Oregon. It's just one thing after another," she said grimly. "Right now I wonder if we shouldn't have stayed in Kansas."

Sick dread washed over Cotton. Not Mama! Beside him, Grandma nodded knowingly. "I said that, I said them very words, myself. But when I said it, everybody acted like I was touched in the head."

He couldn't stand it. "For corn sakes," Cotton blurted, "nobody got hurt but poor old Shag and I bet we can fix him up! Mama, will you look at him while I fill the radiator? Has anybody stopped to think how close we're getting to Rainbow Valley—how soon we're going to see Dad? Well, think about that, and then let's get going. We're not done for yet!"

He saw the slump disappear from Mama's shoulders. A light came to her eyes. "All right, Cotton," she said. "I'm glad to see that the man of this trip still has some starch in his backbone. Fill the radiator. I'll see what I can do for Shag."

Chapter 9
The Un-welcoming

"**I**s he going to be all right?" Cotton asked, watching Mama's gentle fingers exploring Shag's still form lying in the dry grass by the roadside. Mama straightened and brushed her hair away from her face.

"He's still breathing, like you say. There aren't any cuts from the bull's horns, or broken bones. He's unconscious now—if he's only stunned he could come to any time."

Grandma, in a rare moment of gentleness, cut in, "We'll just have to wait and see what happens, Cotton. There's a little water left; we'll keep a wet rag on his head."

Cotton smiled gratefully. He made Shag a bed in the car at his feet. They drove on, through Boise, Nampa, and Caldwell. As the sun went down that night, it was as though the light went out of Cotton also. Shag hadn't moved all day. Cotton slept fitfully on the hard ground, his arm across Shag's warm but unmoving form.

Early next morning, a soft, wet lapping against his right ear brought Cotton awake. "Shag, you're all right boy," he said groggily. He threw an arm around the happily wriggling dog at his side. "Wow, fella," he whispered, his eyes damp, "I wasn't real sure you were going to make it." After a moment, Cotton tossed back his dew-wet quilt and hastily climbed into his overalls. He sniffed deeply of the morning air. "Hey, everybody, wake up!" he yelled, "look at Shag." The dog was on his feet, shaky but alive.

"Don't maul him to death," Cotton laughed a few moments later at his family clustering about Shag. "We have to get going. You kids know we crossed the border into Oregon last night?"

"Now, don't get them excited," Mama chided. "We still have a long way to go—almost four hundred miles to Rainbow Valley."

"Yeah, but we got to Oregon, that's something at least." Cotton grinned. "C'mon, Daisy—Ivy, let's get breakfast ready so we can get moving. Those peaches aren't going to wait all year for us to pick them."

On the road, Cotton watched uneasily as the green fields of corn and sugar beets gave way to barren rimrock and dusty, wide open spaces. All of Oregon couldn't be like this. He'd seen too many pictures of green trees and sparkling rivers.

He settled back. Gosh, he had a lot to be glad about. Shag okay. The Baldwins all going together to a new place where things were going to be a lot better.

His high spirits were still with him when they

stopped at a shabby roadside service station hours later. The others scattered to the restrooms, Shag tail-wagged through the weeds by the side of the road. Cotton hummed, "I wish I was in Dixie—" and limped around the car, kicking the tires to see if they needed air, while the attendant filled the gasoline tank.

"More confounded Okies," a man's angry voice said behind him. "Look at that kid there. Oregon needs people like that like we need more holes in our heads."

"Yeah, we ought to stop 'em from coming here—there ought to be a law," another voice agreed.

Cotton turned idly to see who was being talked about and found two pairs of eyes staring straight at him. He grew uncomfortable. Now what was an 'Okie'? He'd never heard the word before that he could remember. He didn't like it, though. The taller, fancier dressed of the two men sneered at him and spat into the dust.

Cotton looked down at himself. Maybe he did look a sight. His feet were kind of dirty, understandable when a guy had to go without shoes to save them for good. His extra overalls had burned up in the boat fire so he hadn't been able to change into clean ones. But he'd washed up real good in camp this morning. Lightly, he touched his singed eyebrows and eyelashes, and the steam burn on the side of his face. Did Okie mean that—all messed up?

"Say, Mr.—" He limped to where the men lounged against the service station wall. "What's that mean, Okie?"

The men backed away as though he'd just emptied

a bucket of Old Cannibal's feed at their feet. "Get outta' here, Bub," the fat, greasy one snapped.

"G'wan," the taller one gritted. "Blamed white trash brat. Your kind ain't wanted. Cluttering up our schools, down-gradin' our neighborhoods—getting the jobs Oregon folks has a better right to—"

Cotton stopped dead in his tracks, shocked. Neither man had ever laid eyes on him before in his life. They hated him—and they didn't even know him. He whipped about and limped back to the car, his ears ringing with the sneering laughter that followed. "Guess we told one of them off." Cotton recognized the oily voice of the fat man.

"Shag," Cotton called. The dog turned from his foraging and trotted to Cotton's side. "Let's get in the car," Cotton ordered.

"What's the matter, Son?" Mama asked when they were ready to go again. "You look like a house fell on you."

Cotton opened his mouth to tell her what happened, then clamped his lips shut. This he wasn't going to do. He wouldn't tell her they'd gone to a lot of trouble to get here—to a place where they weren't wanted. By some folks, anyway. "Nothing's wrong, Mama," he said, his voice empty, "let's go."

Heat waves danced over the highway before them as morning sped into afternoon. "My, but everybody's quiet," Mama broke the silence inside the car. "I know what will cheer us up. I hate to lose time but I've been thinking we should find a nice, shady park and have a picnic." She quickly raised her voice against the happy clamor that exploded. "The rest and food will do us good. We don't want to look like raggle-taggle strangers to your Dad."

An Okie and a raggle-taggle stranger the same? Cotton wondered bitterly. The picnic idea sounded good, though. Some of the heavy feeling in his chest lifted.

The park they found was only a little cooler than driving on the open highway. Several precious coins went to pay for iced root beer, a loaf of bread, and sliced bologna. Cotton ate with the others in the shade of a battered juniper tree.

"Think I'll look around," he said when he'd finished. He left the others resting on the fenders of the Chevy. Wandering past horseshoe pits and sandbag games, Cotton came to a large can marked "Trash." He turned away sharply from the word, remembering.

He veered wide around families sitting on bright-colored Indian blankets, eating picnic lunches, and stepped gingerly past a ragged hobo stretched out asleep on the ground. Nobody paid him any mind, and he relaxed.

A faint chorus of girls' squeals, boys' hearty laughter, and the sound of splashing water came to his ears as he walked. Cotton grinned as the noise grew louder. A swimming pool! He came to the fenced pool at the far end of the park. Many of the boys and girls who churned the green waters to a white froth were his age. Cotton moved closer to watch.

A boy in yellow swim trunks, round and golden as a ball of butter, danced out to the end of the diving board, executed all the motions of a beautiful dive, then landed in the pool with a comic, horrible, belly-flop. Cotton's laugh rang out with the others.

The water sure would feel good. Cotton wiped the sweat from his forehead with his bare arm and limped to the small green building where three girls handed over dripping suits. "Does it cost much to swim?" he asked the attendant behind the counter. The man jerked a thumb at a sign behind his head. Cotton looked, and shook his head in disappointment. Close behind him, a voice, smooth as cornsilk, spoke.

"They don't let dirty Okies swim here, anyhow."

Cotton whirled to face a dark, handsome boy dressed in a dazzling shirt and shorts. He let himself be pushed aside as the boy arrogantly tossed a wet suit at the attendant's back, saying, "Catch, Sam."

"Some day somebody's going to teach you some manners, Ted Lassiter," the attendant barked. He grabbed a towel and rubbed furiously at the back of his neck where the suit had struck.

The boy named Ted laughed, showing even, white teeth. Suddenly, he whirled on Cotton. "Hey, hick, what you staring at? You looking for something?"

"Yep," Cotton made his voice calm, "I'm looking for somebody to explain a word to me. Okie. You look like a smart guy. Maybe you can tell me what it means."

"An Okie, my stupid friend, is a dumb kid like you. Okies are white trash. Stinking, dirty tramps from Oklahoma."

Cotton itched to smash his fist into the handsome,

sweaty nose only an inch from his own. What would that prove, though? He stepped back and hooked his thumbs under his suspenders. "I'm from Kansas," he said quietly. "And my folks and me aren't tramps or trash. We had a farm of our own till we got dusted out. An' as far as folks from Oklahoma are concerned, I got a feeling they are as good as you, any day. S'long, governor." Cotton turned to leave.

He took two steps, saw the flash of Ted Lassiter's foot, tried to step aside. Pain jabbed his left shin as he was tripped; the ground slammed up to meet him. He climbed to his feet, gasping. His hands clenched into fists.

"Cotton!" a frightened voice cried behind him, "stop!" Daisy ran toward him. "Mama said for you to come. We're ready to go." She looked fearfully at Lassiter who stood smirking at them.

Cotton wavered. Mama wouldn't like it if he fought. Grandma neither. They claimed a man was given good sense so he wouldn't have to fight like an animal. He'd sure like to pound some sense into this Lassiter, though. He'd had enough trouble on this trip —he hadn't expected to be called names for no reason at all—and it made him madder than a bee in a bottle.

"Please, Cotton. Let's go," Daisy pleaded.

"All right," Cotton sighed. Disappointment lay in his stomach like a lump of sickness. He gave one last level look at Lassiter, then hurried after Daisy.

A wave of laughter followed them. Cotton brushed the dirt and twigs from the front of his overalls.

"Hey, Okie, did your sister come to take you bye-

bye? What are you brushing the dirt off for? A little more isn't going to make any difference on you."

"Don't pay any attention, Cotton," Daisy begged. "He's just trying to get you mad so you'll fight."

Cotton gritted his teeth and didn't answer. He held his steps slow and deliberate as Ted Lassiter charged up and fell in beside him.

"You know, Okie," Lassiter said, "you're acting kind of stuck up for white trash." He came around in front of them, dancing on his toes like a boxer. Taking his towel in his right hand, he twisted it with his left until it resembled a thick snake. With a quick twist of his wrist, he snapped it sharply against the bib of Cotton's overalls.

Cotton saw him aim next at Daisy's bare legs. Moving lightning-swift, Cotton caught the end of the snapping towel in mid-air and yanked it backward hard. He leaped aside to let the other boy fly by him of balance. "Run!" Cotton cried. He grabbed Daisy's arm and pulled her along.

Suddenly the laughing crowd gasped. Cotton whirled to look. He froze, seeing the horseshoe leave Ted Lassiter's hand to whizz straight at him. Cotton ducked.

The horseshoe thudded. A quick, sharp scream rang out. Horror washed over Cotton. He turned to see Daisy crumple and fall like a broken doll. He ran and fell to his knees beside her. "Daisy," he choked, "Daisy."

Chapter 10
Cotton Confesses

The crowd quickly closed in around them. "I didn't mean to hurt her, I didn't mean to," a voice Cotton recognized as Ted Lassiter's kept repeating. Cotton looked up dazed. The other boy was pale.

Cotton watched Ted Lassiter disappear, shoving his way through the crowd. He slipped an arm under Daisy's neck and felt a wetness on his arm. "Daisy?" he cried. Blood oozed onto his arm from the back of her head. "Daisy!" he shouted.

He sighed with relief as her eyes fluttered open. "Wh-what happened?" she asked weakly. "Ooo—oo, my head hurts."

Above Cotton, a husky voice asked, "Want I should get a doctor, kid?" Cotton looked up and saw the tattered hobo who had been sleeping.

"She's my sister," Cotton answered, "I'll take care of her." He asked Daisy, "Can you stand?" She nodded and he helped her carefully to her feet. They moved slowly. Over his shoulder, Cotton said to the old man, "Thanks anyway, sir."

"Does it hurt bad?" Cotton asked.

Daisy shook her head, her smile wobbly. "N-n-not t-t-too bad."

Cotton kept his arm around her to steady her as they moved through the park. "We're almost to the car," he said finally, and added, "I'm sorry, Sis."

Guilt tightened Cotton's throat when he saw Mama running toward them.

"What on earth happened?" she asked. They helped Daisy to the running board where she sat down.

"It wasn't Cotton's fault," Daisy interrupted as Cotton told what happened. "The other boy wouldn't leave him alone."

Cotton chewed his lip as Mama gently examined the cut on the back of Daisy's head. "It isn't too bad," she sighed, her hand on Daisy's shoulder, "but it will need a few stitches. All right, everybody in the car. We'll look for a doctor."

Worry needled Cotton as they drove slowly along Main Street. Daisy needed a doctor, and he wanted her to have one. But how much would the doctor charge? Would there be enough left over to get them to Dad? His throat was dry. He had to tell them about the bow and quiver. Now. He cleared his throat and blurted, "Mama, I have to tell you something."

"Later, Cotton," she scolded, "I have enough on my mind just now. Look, there's a doctor's office. I see the sign. My," she worried, "I hope he won't be expensive. Have your money handy, Cotton." They pulled to a stop before a small white building.

Cotton opened his mouth to speak again, then closed it quickly. Further down the street was a gray, spraddling building that looked about to collapse. A faded sign proclaimed, ANNIE'S SECOND-HAND— WE BUY AND SELL. Maybe—"I'll wait outside," he announced.

Cotton stood beside the car, heart pounding, waiting. The others disappeared into the doctor's office. Moving fast, he clawed the back seat out, got the bow and quiver, and shoved the seat back into place. Seconds later he hurried down the street, the bow gripped tightly in one hand, the quiver in the other. Shag trotted beside him.

The windows of the second-hand store were dirty. He could hardly see inside. A bell tinkled as he opened the door. "Wait outside, boy," he told Shag. The bare boards of the floor shook as a woman in a purple dress waddled toward him. He held the bow and quiver out for her to see. "I-I want to sell these," he croaked finally.

"Real, huh?" the woman asked in a deep, rasping voice.

Cotton nodded. "Pawnee. I have to have at least ten dollars for 'em."

The woman shook her head, her chins wobbling. "I couldn't spare it, not even for a beautiful set like that." Her fat hand patted his shoulder. "Sorry."

"Th-that's all right," Cotton said, greatly relieved. Was he crazy? he wondered in the next instant. He had to sell the bow. As he turned away, the woman spoke.

"Say, now, just a minute. The cafe across the street has Indian and western stuff all over the place," she said. "Homer, the owner, collects it. Don't know if he wants any more relics, but he's the only one I can think of."

Cotton thanked her and hurried from the store.

The cafe smelled strongly of coffee and fried onions. Cotton hesitated in the doorway, then moved slowly to the counter, the bow and quiver gripped tightly in his sweating hands. He glanced about. A huge yoke hung on a side wall above a booth. Stone-head tomahawks hung at each end of the yoke. Glass-enclosed picture boxes containing Indian beadwork, arrowheads, and wampum were scattered about the walls.

A hawk-faced man with a thatch of white hair wiped at the counter in front of him. "What have you got there, fella?" He nodded at the bow.

Although he couldn't have said why, Cotton didn't like the man looking greedily at the bow and quiver. "Are y-you Homer, sir?" Cotton asked, his heart hammering in his throat.

The man nodded and reached for the bow.

Cotton held it out. His fingers loosened slowly. "The l-lady a-across the street said you might buy it," he stammered. "It's real Pawnee. A Chief gave it to my Grandpa 'cause Grandpa saved the women and children of the tribe from starving." Cotton's tongue felt leaden as he asked, "Do—you want it?"

The man rubbed his palm expertly along the curve of the bow. "It'll do," he said. He eyed Cotton. "You look like you might be hungry, fella. Tell you what I'll do. You can have a hot meal here every day for two weeks—for the bow and quiver."

Cotton stepped back, shaking his head. He reached for the bow. The man drew it back out of his reach.

"I-I need money," Cotton finally got out, alarm building inside him. "I can't take anything else. Can't you let me have ten dollars for them? They're worth it, easy."

"Not to me," the man grunted. "No cash. Meals, or nothing."

"We're just passing through," Cotton explained. "We need money for gasoline to take us the rest of the way to Gladrock, in Rainbow Valley. And we need money to buy food for the whole family. I-I better take them," he said, reaching again for the bow and quiver.

"Take 'em then," the man snorted, his face knotting into ugly bumps. "G'wan, scram!"

Cotton took the bow and quiver and stumbled from the cafe. What could he do now? His family would be looking for him.

They were still inside when he arrived at the doctor's office. Cotton dropped to the front steps and sat with the bow and quiver across his knees. Shag lay at his feet, looking up at him solemnly. A choked feeling threatened to stifle Cotton's breathing. He'd fixed things good. Unless—unless the doctor wouldn't charge a terrible lot. Maybe—maybe, they would still have enough money to reach Dad. It wasn't far to Rainbow Valley.

The office door opened suddenly behind him. Cotton jumped to his feet and stood out of the way. Daisy came out first, her head bound by a snowy bandage. Ivy followed. Her eyes widened as she saw the bow and quiver in Cotton's hands. "That's the—" she started to say, then suddenly clapped a hand over her mouth as though she didn't want to voice the news that was sure to spell trouble for Cotton.

Grandma Baldwin came next, leading Bobby, followed by Mama carrying Kurt. They stood on the steps staring at him. Cotton wanted to run, to escape the shock and disappointment in their faces.

Instead, he swallowed and stood straighter in an effort to gain courage for what he wanted to say. "I-I'm sorry, Mama," he began. "But I thought I ought to keep the bow and quiver because they—they were Grandpa's. It seemed more important to have them than— money we might not need. I thought I could get us to Dad no matter what. And I tried—"

It was Grandma who interrupted. Cotton could hardly believe his ears! She sounded so happy and— strong. "Cotton did right," she declared. "His Grandpa thought of lot of that bow and quiver, too. That's why he gave 'em to Cotton. He never would've wanted him to use them as an easy way out of trouble. They're a man's trappings—an' durned if I don't think the boy's earned 'em. Don't you give up now, Cotton. You can get us to that blamed valley!"

Cotton tried to say something, thank her, but he

couldn't find his voice. He led the way down the steps and hurried to open the car door for Grandma. Through the mist in his eyes he saw her grin.

Nobody spoke as they climbed into the car. Mama leaned against the steering wheel, her head in her arms. "I'm sorry I let you down, Mama. I have this idea, though—to get us to Dad—"

Mama looked up and smiled, but he could see worry in her eyes. "Grandma's right about the bow and quiver, Son," she said. "But I just gave the doctor the last penny I had. I don't even have enough money to call your daddy and tell him what happened."

"My idea, Mama, please, listen. We filled the gasoline tank just before the picnic, remember? That will take us quite a ways. I figure it is only about a hundred or so miles to Gladrock. Maybe we can get all the way there, or close enough so I can walk the rest of the way and find Dad." Cotton waited hopefully for her reaction.

Several seconds ticked by. Finally, she shook her head. "All right, Cotton. As your father has often said, 'Nothing works 'til it's tried.' And there isn't anything else we can do."

"Let's sing to make the time go faster," Daisy suggested when they were again on the highway. "Home, home on the range—" she began in a high sweet voice.

"Hey, that's my song," Cotton laughed. He joined in loudly. Soon the whole family was singing. The baby, Kurt, added his "M-m-m's" to the traditional words, rocking to and fro in Daisy's lap.

As he sang, Cotton felt glad enough to fly. The others knew about the bow at last. It was as though a huge stone had been lifted from him.

They'd make it to Rainbow Valley, where Dad was waiting for them. They had to. In a few hours—just hours—not days, they would be there! In his mind's eye, Cotton saw his father—tall and thin from his battle with dust and hard times—but quick to laugh, or hug, or tease. As though she were reading his mind, Mama said, "Let's sing Daddy's favorite song."

No one hesitated. "Glory, glory hallelujah," they sang, their voices filling the car with joy, and hope. "Glory, glory hallelujah. Glory, glory hallelujah, his truth is marching on."

Chapter 11
The Promised Valley

They had crossed the McKenzie Pass. The snowy peaks of the Three Sisters mountains were behind them. Cotton sang until his throat ached. One by one the others stopped singing. Finally, Cotton, too, fell silent.

It was cool. Outside a massive wall of giant evergreen trees lined each side of the highway and above them he could see a patch of blue. But Cotton could not look for long at the scenery. He fastened his gaze on the needle of the gas gauge as it moved nearer and nearer the red "empty" mark.

Ten minutes went by. Fifteen. As the needle signaled empty, his stomach knotted. A few miles further the engine coughed, the car slowed, and stopped. Cotton made a swift decision.

"Now, Mama, don't worry," he said. "Let me out of the car. I'll flag somebody to stop."

"Flag somebody!" Mama cried. "Cotton, I've never

seen such a deserted stretch of road. We haven't seen another car in the last hour."

"I'll think it out, Mama, I'll figure it out," Cotton said sheepishly. "Somehow we'll get hold of Dad and let him know where we are."

They climbed from the car. Daisy spread a blanket in the soft needles under a fir tree by the side of the road. Ivy and the little boys joined her and were soon busy building castles of cones.

Cotton limped back and forth along the roadside, Shag pacing with him. Grandma and Mama sat in the car, doors open, talking in worried tones. If someone would only come this way, Cotton thought, and give him a lift to a house or a store where he could use a telephone, he'd call Dad. Dad would find a way to come get them, he knew.

Time crawled by. Finally, Cotton heard a sound like distant thunder. He cupped a hand behind his ear.

"Yippee!" he shouted. "A car is coming!" Cotton waited eagerly for it to reach them.

Seconds later a shiny black automobile was whizzing down on him. Cotton waved his arms frantically, motioning it to stop. It roared by, the driver not even looking in his direction.

Thoroughly disgusted, Cotton gouged the road dust with his big toe, and began his limping vigil again.

Much later, a battered pickup came rattling down the road, shaking like it had some disease of old age. Cotton rushed toward it, swinging his arms back and forth in an arc. "Stop!" he yelled. "Please stop, mister."

The pickup slowed and stopped in the middle of

the highway. Cotton's heart leaped. He started to cross to the pickup, then stopped short. The driver, a dark mountain of a man, made Cotton think of a gorilla. His expression through the open window was one of anger and dislike.

"Serves you Okies right," the man barked. His swarthy jaws wobbled, "Should have stayed where you belonged."

Cotton remained motionless, feeling sick. Here it was again.

The pickup coughed and sputtered on down the highway, Cotton staring after it, his arms limp at his sides.

"Son," Mama called from the car. "What did that man call us?"

It was bound to happen. He had hoped the rest of the family wouldn't find out they weren't wanted in Oregon. Until they were with Dad, anyway. Reluctantly, Cotton went to her and explained. "He called us Okies, Mama. I don't know for sure, but I think that's what folks out here call people from Oklahoma. They think Okies, whatever that is, aren't as good as other people."

With downcast eyes, he choked out, "I guess they want to keep Oregon for themselves. They think we should've stayed put."

To his surprise, Mama laughed. Softly, but sad, too. "The foolish notions some people have," she said. Her work-worn hand reached for his own grubby fingers. "I suppose Okies are folks like us. Driven off their land by dust and drought. Seems to me, though, it would make more sense to be mad at the cause of these folks' troubles—not the unfortunate souls themselves. And when a family sets out to better its lot, no matter where they are from, or where they're going, others will benefit, too."

"Like the pioneers who came here to Oregon a long time ago," Cotton nodded, beginning to understand. "Or the Pilgrims on the Mayflower."

Mama laughed. "That man probably doesn't think about it, but his people were newcomers here once."

Relief flooded Cotton. It was as though Mama's words had suddenly washed him clean. He made room for Ivy who had come to lean against Mama's knee while they were talking.

"I know what you mean, Mama," Ivy said. "In school we learned that 'America is the melting pot of the world.' That means all kinds of people live here."

Cotton hooked his thumbs under his suspenders. Things were okay again. But they were wasting time. "Mama," he said, "let's don't wait any longer. It can't be more than fifteen or twenty miles to Rainbow Valley. I can find a house and telephone Dad. I know he'd be here to get us, quicker than anything."

Mama hesitated, looking eager, then worried, then eager again. Finally, she spoke. "It may be ten miles to the nearest house. But you'd better go. It'll be dark soon," she fretted. "We—we'll pray that you find a farm right away. Cotton, if anything happened to you, I don't know—"

Afraid she might change her mind, Cotton gave her a quick grin and started off. "Keep Shag here, for protection," he called back over his shoulder, taking long hopping strides down the highway. After a while he broke into a clumsy, limping trot, anxious to shorten the time and distance between himself and Dad.

A few cars came along, none stopped. The sky over the darkening timber to the west turned yellow, then apricot, and finally purple as the sun sank out of sight. Still, Cotton saw no houses. Dusk turned to dark as he limped on, an aching weariness settling in his legs. How far had he walked? He had no idea.

He forced one numb leg to follow the other. Back at the car, they would be afraid, stranded in the dark on the lonely road. He had to reach Dad, soon.

Much later, he saw a spark of light through half-closed lids. Like a robot, he turned off the road toward it. He stumbled into a fence, fell, got up, climbed the fence, and kept going. The spark grew in size. From far off, in the direction of the light, a dog barked. Cotton made himself move faster. The barking of the dog grew louder. At last, the spark became a wide shaft of light as someone opened a door.

"Who is out there?" a voice called.

"Here," Cotton croaked, "out here." Moments later he was being led into a bright, cheery room. A man and woman, their ruddy faces filled with kindness, urged him to sit on a fat, plum-colored sofa.

Cotton sat down and poured out his story.

When he finished, the eyes of the farm wife were bright with tears. She pointed to a black box on the wall. "There's the telephone. Call your daddy. Go ahead."

Cotton got up and went to the phone. He studied it, then the pink flowers on the pale green wallpaper. He spread his hands helplessly. "I don't know what to do. I never used a telephone before."

The sun-browned farmer was at his side in an instant, grabbing the handle at the side of the phone. He gave it a quick turn. Waited. "Central," he said into the mouthpiece, "you get me—" he turned to Cotton, "what's your daddy's name?"

Cotton told him and the man turned back to the phone. "Get Mr. Preston Baldwin, Gladrock. It's important, Central."

The farmer shoved the receiver into Cotton's hand and pushed him toward the mouthpiece. Cotton held the receiver to his ear gingerly. His knees felt as cold and watery as melting snow. From inside the receiver he could hear buzzing noises, then a ringing. A voice suddenly jumped out at him. Cotton leaped back from the telephone.

"Hello! Hello!" said the familiar voice. "Who's there?"

Cotton's eyes widened. It was Dad. He moved up to the mouthpiece and shouted, "Me. I'm here. Cotton. George Baldwin. You know, your son!"

"Cotton!" Dad's voice was gleeful. "Where are you, Son? What's happened? Is everyone all right?"

"We're fine, Dad," Cotton answered. "We did run out of gas—and—and money. I walked to this farmer's house to telephone you to come get us. I don't think we're more than nine or ten miles from you."

"Great, Son," Dad boomed. "Now let me talk to the fellow whose house you're calling from. I'd like to get directions from him on how to find you. Our neighbor will loan me his truck to come get you."

The farmer took Cotton's place at the telephone. "Meet us here," he told Dad, after giving directions, "the boy and I will go out and bring your family in."

At first, Mama and Grandma were reluctant to be a burden and refused to come. At last they gave in and back at the farm, the farmer's wife soon hushed their apologies and coaxed the family to a huge table in the kitchen where she had set out a meal of leftover chicken, fluffy dumplings, sliced tomatoes, milk, and golden-crusted wild blackberry pie.

Cotton ate to bursting. What wonderful people these Oregon folks are! he thought. At that instant, a knock sounded at the front door.

"I'll get it," the farmer said, beaming.

"Daddy!" the glad cry rang out. And there he was, coming out of the dark through the open door, arms outstretched, a wide grin on his face, shouting, "Ha! My family!"

There was a wild shuffle as Dad was ambushed in a welter of kisses and hugs. Cotton stood back, grinning until his jaws ached, a lump as big as an apple in his throat. A moment later, Dad was reaching out, clasping his shoulder. "Son," he said, his smile warm. He whistled. "Looks like you've been through a war,

Cotton. I want you to tell me all about it when we get home."

The farmer and his wife offered their upstairs bedrooms for the rest of the night. Cotton was glad when his parents declined. None of the Baldwins wanted to postpone reaching their new home a single, unnecessary minute. It was decided they would return for the Chevy with the neighbor in his truck tomorrow.

Dawn spilled a rosy glow over the tall white farmhouse as they drove through the front gate. Cotton climbed down from the back of the truck. He helped the others down. Standing with his hand resting on Shag's head, Cotton looked and looked, a feeling of gladness flowing into every inch of his body. He'd never forget this minute, ever.

Rose bushes, laden with blossoms of red, pink, white and yellow fenced in the green front yard. A wooden walk led to the wide porch that ran around three sides of the gabled house. Behind the house he could see sturdy sheds, a big red barn, and further still, low, rolling hills with row upon neat row of peach trees that seemed to go on forever.

He sighed deeply. So he looked like he'd been through a war? The trip had been sort of like a war, almost as exciting as a Jack London adventure. He was glad it was over, though. And glad he'd won the war!

He watched the girls and Bobby race to the end of the yard. "A fish pond!" they squealed happily, hopping up and down, "with real goldfish in it!"

Kurt scooted from his mother's arms to bury his face deep in a pink cabbage rose blooming by the front steps. Grandma's eyes were lit with pleasure. "I never thought it'd be so fancy-fine as this," she crowed.

Mama, held tight in the circle of Dad's arm, laughed and cried at the same time. "Oh, Pres, oh, Pres," she said over and over.

It was several seconds before Cotton realized Dad had turned and was waiting for him with his right hand outstretched. Cotton joined them. "Your Mama has been telling me how you managed things, getting out here," Dad said. "We both figure a grown man couldn't have done any better."

Cotton answered Dad's warm handshake with a firm grip and grinned. At that moment he realized a new road was stretching out before him—as a man, alongside Dad. They'd work the new farm—hunt, fish, all sorts of wonderful things, together. A happier time ahead he couldn't imagine.

A look at: Morning Glory Afternoon

Experience the captivating journey of 17-year-old Jessamyn Faber in *Morning Glory Afternoon,* a thrilling YA Western coming-of-age novel.

Transport yourself to 1924 Ardensville, Kansas, where Jessy arrives with a hidden sorrow in her heart. Seeking solace from her past, she embarks on a job as the indispensable but anonymous telephone operator, known as "Central."

As Jessy assumes her role, she becomes the epicenter of the town's gossip, drama, and emergencies. Unbeknownst to the tranquil façade, Ardensville harbors deep-rooted issues. A group of townspeople relentlessly persecutes those who are different, including Jessy's own friends. A menacing organization emerges, wreaking havoc on the town.

Join Jessy on an extraordinary quest as she musters the unforeseen strength within herself to confront Ardensville's pressing challenges. *Morning Glory Afternoon* is not just an exhilarating adventure but also an uplifting coming-of-age romance set in the vibrant backdrop of the Wild West. Delve into this inspiring tale that explores themes of resilience, love, and social consciousness.

AVAILABLE FEBRUARY 2024

About the Author

Irene Bennett Brown is an award-winning author who enjoys using Kansas—where she was born—as background for her historical novels. Previous to her ten novels for adults, Brown authored nine young adult novels. *Before the Lark* won a Western Writers of America Spur Award, was nominated for the Mark Twain Award, and received other honors. Her other YA novels include *To Rainbow Valley, Run from a Scarecrow, Skitterbrain, Willow Whip, Morning Glory Afternoon, Answer Me Answer Me, I Loved You Logan McGee, and Just Another Gorgeous Guy.*

Her most recent Nickel Hill series include *Miss Royal's Mules, Tangled Times, Somebody's Business* and *One True Deed.* All are adult sequels to *Before the Lark.*

She lives with her husband, Bob—a retired research chemist—on two fruitful acres along the Santiam River in Oregon.

Visit her website at irenebennettbrown.net for more information.